DEPRIVATIONAL MEAN

A Pick of the Litter

by Cory Perala

authorHOUSE®

AuthorHouse™
1663 Liberty Drive
Bloomington, IN 47403
www.authorhouse.com
Phone: 1-800-839-8640

Published by AuthorHouse 5/8/2013

ISBN: 978-1-4817-5078-3 (sc)
ISBN: 978-1-4817-5077-6 (e)

Library of Congress Control Number: 2013908239

CHAPTER 1

On a foggy spring morning in a parking lot outside of Don's Coffee Shop in Trenton, Minnesota, the fog fades out the shop's red sign. The sun has yet to rise and the "early birds" or morning regulars are inside conversing about the day's top headlines. A man named Roy is inside drinking a dark caffeinated coffee, just what he needs to prepare for his very long day. He sits at his usual table in the middle of the elongated dining area in between two social groups.

The Coffee shop has a group of four females in their thirties sitting at a table by the back exit. High stool chairs and tables are at the front entrance where five old gentlemen talk about how times have changed.

The man in the green hooded sweatshirt says, "When I was young I used to walk over hills and through cold winter storms to get to school. Now look, kids are driving to school in new cars."

A man across the table in a John Deere cap responds with a smile, "Yeah Jim, but how many school days did you actually show up for school?"

The coffee shop worker is heard grinding a special blend of coffee beans. Each time the coffee grinder turns on the worker's mustache shudders from vibrations transferring throughout his body while holding onto the vibrating coffee machine.

The group of ladies at the back exit sit preparing their make up with hand held mirrors. One takes a sip of her coffee and shouts, "Yikes! That is hot, not prepared for that!"

The lady across the table from her exchanges a few words over to the shop worker, "The freshest coffee is the hottest right Jake?"

"That's right" says Jake talking loud enough to be heard over the sound of the coffee grinder. "Adding a little sugar or cream will not be enough to tame the heat of my fresh cup of coffee."

"I guess we will have to start coming later to let the coffee have time to cool", replies the black haired woman who burnt herself with the coffee.

Jake replies, "Uh, I will make a separate batch that is milder from now on. The coffee should be ready in time for when you show up Sue."

Roy is about half way into his cup of coffee staring at his employer's monthly newsletter covering recent performances within the past year. Roy has his usual flannel shirt, which fits loosely to his tall skinny body type. His front cowlick makes the short brown hair style heavy to the left. Next, the front door bell rings to signal a new customer walking into the shop. The person is a female in her thirties with blonde hair, long bangs that curl out to touch her front forehead, and small diamond earrings. Roy notices the woman at first glance with a look of lucky recognition in his face. A handful of thoughts and memories run through Roy's mind while he waits to choose the right words in getting the blonde's attention.

The new customer walks her short and small frame to the cash register table and orders a cappuccino from the owner. When the purchase is being made for the cappuccino the woman smiles and hands over three dollars for the two dollars and thirteen cent cappuccino. After receiving the eighty seven cents in change, the blonde turns to look for a seat.

"Amanda what does this new day bring you?" Roy says in an energetic tone to the blonde with a fresh cappuccino. Amanda recognizes the voice and looks at Roy sitting at the table about ten feet away.

With an expression of amazement Amanda says, "Roy, it's so good to see you. Has it been ten years since we last met?"

Roy replies, "Since college graduation from my memory."

"Wow what is new with you? Where do you live? Where do you work?" says Amanda.

"Take a seat and we will catch up on the past ten years" says Roy.

"Great, I have a lot of time on my hands as I have today off from work," says Amanda pulling out the cushioned chair that is tightly tucked under the table and sits down lazily by letting her legs give out from under her. Putting her black leather purse on the tucked in chair next to her, she takes a moment to get comfortable by shrugging her shoulders once while rearranging her hips on the seat. Amanda says, "the last words I remember you telling me are: live well and prosper."

Roy replies with a smile, "well how have you done for your self?"

"I guess alright, after college I did what I intended with managing my father's corporation, married Sam and added two children to the picture," says Amanda.

Roy adds in while looking directly in Amanda's eyes, "Destiny may have had an influence in those occurrences. Would you agree?"

Amanda answers as if making an excuse, "Yes I see the point you are making, but nothing is free, either way work is work." Turning the position of her coffee on the table so the mouth spout is facing her, she takes two sips while looking to the right outside the dark windows.

"On the topic of destiny, where did that pick of the litter get you?" Amanda asks while looking down at her coffee.

"Yes I obtained a job with my degree sooner or later for sales and marketing at Canet Lights," says Roy.

"Oh, the life of fashion and luxury appeals to you also," says Amanda.

Coming to the end of his coffee grinding, Jake heads to the back for his next routine task. Roy looks over Amanda's shoulder at the next customer to enter the shop, a business man in a suit and tie. "So how do I look since we last met?" Roy asks while looking at the business man as if envying him.

Amanda says without hesitation, "Uh, you look well in spirit with a great outlook."

Roy says, "That is a fraction of my story, these circles that I wear under my eyes are shades of difficulty overlapped by optimism and hope. Much of what I do and how I look now is part destiny and part of my decision making." A twitch in his eye signals a visual flashback of a dark and cold experience.

4

The number of people in the coffee shop starts to grow and grow as the morning rush hour nears. Jake is now busy servicing customers with coffee and pastries, having a long awaited facial expression for this kind of business.

Roy includes, "So how long up the ladder have you climbed since the pick of the litter after college?"

Amanda responds, "I do not know, let's start with you first, then I will share my experience in return." Roy's facial expression turns pale with his mouth dropped open and looking at Amanda's coffee. His eyes shudder side to side, recalling his past and searching where to begin his story.

Chapter 2

As we both know, upon graduating from college in the days of the early 2000s' there were not many job openings available due to our local economy. The first couple of months were better than I expected with the opportunity of three job interviews: one at a retail warehouse and two at the local newspaper office. Of course they said I got turned down due to the better applicant having either more experience or connections with employees that work there. I continued my work at the Chester's Chicken as an evening delivery driver with no intentions to make the job a career. I did not want to risk moving to a bigger city even though I had enough money, the risk did not out weigh the benefit of a low paying entry level job I would get with my degree at the time.

The fourth job interview came eight months later as I continued to apply for jobs in the meantime with no interview offers. The company was Canet, a maker of light bulbs increasing production with LED and High Efficiency Lights. The position called for marketing and selling the lights to outdoor retailers and sporting arenas under contract. Even though the pay started out at fifty cents above minimum wage, I took the job due to being out of my college loan grace period for two months and needing some practice in my profession. I was glad about the full time position with benefits.

My first day was interesting with a competitive working climate Erik and Rinae created. We had sales goals and bonuses based on our performance, which motivated me to use the aggressive selling tools I had learned in school. First impressions are always the most important with establishing relationships, right? Well, this was not that smooth.

"Hi, my name is Roy Monte." Roy says while standing above Erik sitting in his office chair and extending his arm towards Erik for a hand shake.

Erik expresses a wide smile and connects with Roy's hand with a firm handshake. "You're Roy, nice to meet you, one question: when selling to large buyers, would you first try to negotiate at average market price or above market price?"

"Average market price," says Roy "to give a better offer than our larger competitors and selling more product will increase work for our production lines." Showing confidence in his answer he notices Erik wincing his brown eyes, which makes his bald head stretch forward and puffy cheeks rise. Erik's short and wide frame makes Roy look like a tall flag poll with a basket ball hoop next to it.

While glancing over to Rinae, Erik says, "Wrong, our philosophy is to get above average market price due today's light bulb lasting much longer with High Efficiency. You see when retailer and entertainment facilities buy lights; they buy in bulk to get a better price. When we start negotiating above market price, there are more possibilities to generate profit with bargaining the contract agreement."

"I see, you are saying that the price will be similar with

either negotiating strategy due to the fact the buyer has shopped around for quotes with our competitors. Negotiating at a higher price to start with will give more opportunity for our customers to think they are getting a good deal." Roy says to make sure he is on the right page with Erik.

Rinae swivel's in her chair to square her shoulders at the two men and lifts up the Canet Catalog. Her clothes make her body frame look thin while having grey dress pants and a black button up dress shirt. With her brown hair in a pony tail and blond highlights show symmetry to indicate an intentional fashion.

Rinae asks Erik, "Is there anything else to let Roy know about for add-ons at the point of purchase?"

"Yes, throw in a Canet Light Bulb Life Expectancy Tester and a free Canet Pocket LED Light for every employee at the purchasing company to finalize the deal," Erik answers with a determined set of eye brows slanting inward.

Living the moment of making a deal is something that Erik thrives on. His selling style includes asking for a high price and negotiating at a final price of ten to fifteen percent less with added features to make customer's think about the good deal. Working under Erik and Rinae would be a very good learning experience in the marketing and selling field. Ah, my first business contact came within the next few minutes as I sat down with my contact list of buyers inquiring for Canet's business. Of course, this was my chance to make things happen with a large potential buyer at a home improvement store. I called the number and squeezed the phone in between my shoulder and chin while holding a paper and pencil in hand to take notes.

"Hello, this is Sangard Home Improvement, how may I help you," the voice on the other line said.

"Yes, this is Roy with Canet Lights; we received an inquiry about our fluorescents lights. May I speak with Cameron please?" says Roy as if he's dealt with the company before.

"Yes, one moment please as I put you on hold," says the person answering Roy's call.

A few seconds later, the phone picks up. "Cameron here, what can I do for you?" says Cameron.

"Cameron, this is Roy with Canet Lights. I'm calling about the quote you requested yesterday afternoon." Now, Roy is preparing for his gradual climb of negotiating by breaking the ice. "Cameron, how much is your electric bill each month for the location you work at?" says Roy.

"Thirteen hundred a month, this is consistent all year round," Cameron says with confidence and a tone of voice that is curious to see what Canet can do for him.

Roy engages Cameron by getting to the point saying, "Our new E8000 florescent lights will cost you less in monthly expenses by the crystal glass material in their design. Crystal glass actually duplicates the brightness of the light, producing more light with less electricity. Today, these lights are at a price of $250 per case."

"Uh, General Electric just quoted me with a similar product at a lower price that is fixed under our pending contract." Cameron says with an uninterested tone of voice, which makes Roy's eyes widen.

Rinae is looking at Roy now and can tell the shift in Roy's facial expression upon hearing the buyer's response. She whispers with a smile, "Use fear as fuel Roy." Roy pauses his response with Cameron upon hearing Rinae in order to try and incorporate the meaning of fear as fuel into the conversation.

"Have you been informed of General Electric's recent recall on their fluorescent lights due to a loose attachment base?" Roy says to counter the competitor's quote.

"They did not tell me this," say Cameron.

Roy adds in, "Cameron, Sangard is running low on florescent lights, would it be wise to purchase lights that have been fixed and not proven in the field. There is a potential for another recall and then Sangard has stores that are half lit due to waiting weeks for new lights to return. How does $220 per case sound with our light having a 2 year four out of five star rating from customers?"

Cameron pauses in his response for more than a few seconds and responds with a tone of voice that Roy can tell is identical to Cameron's smiling greet, "I like where you're going with this Roy. Looking at my computer now, I do confirm the truth about General Electric's recall."

"I'll throw in a Pocket Canet LED Light for every Employee at your store and send contract papers to your fax. This fixed term contract lasts for ten years and includes an adjustable purchase amount based on need. How long was General Electric's proposed contract term?" says Roy with a grin on his face.

Rinae still looks over her shoulder at Roy in an office room which is a horse shoe ring of cubicles. Raised eyebrows indicate her surprise with a lucky first caller. Erik not being surprised, has many tasks being worked on with five different files being shuffled like playing cards.

Cameron says, "I'll take your price at $220 a case and

fax the papers completed this afternoon. I'll look forward to doing business with Canet in the future. Have a good day."

"You too Cameron and thank you for your time," says Roy with reassurance before Cameron hangs up the phone.

Roy hangs up the phone with a happy smile on his face and looks over to Rinae and asks, "Is that what you meant as using fear as fuel?"

Rinae responds, "Right on target."

Erik adds in while writing notes in his work files, "Just keep it rolling and we'll be on top with the big wigs."

"I like the sound of that, Woo Hoo!" Jamie sounds in with enthusiasm and confidence. While pumping her fists in the air and smiling, her head nods twice vigorously to make her pony tail whip lash like the crack of a whip.

By the end of the day, Roy goes through a list of twenty contacts and is able to make a sale on four of them. Not good enough for Roy, he knows he can do better. In the next few days, a sale is made on five percent of Roy's contacts. The goal was around ten to fifteen percent, which Rinae was the only one able to do this most often.

***

Two weeks later, the March Madness Canet Lights Promotion takes place, and Roy is working on a couple of three month projects the company manager assigns for new offerings. One is Christmas Lights and the other was a proposal for selling lights to the city of New York at the New Years Eve Times Square Light Show. One week is the amount of time given to present ideas to company officials.

The day before the presentation, Erik has just finished his usual two hours of sales calls with current customers when he asks Roy, "In a test of time management, will a Cheetah or an Elephant have a better score? Assume the cheetah works fast with breaks to produce high volume of work in streaks and the elephant works slow and consistently."

Roy includes, "The cheetah works quick for a while and takes a brake to think over what he has done and where he is going, while the elephant has more time to choose with working at a slower pace. Depends on the situation, either could be the right working philosophy."

"I see the cheetah being more risky with bigger potential pay offs in the long run pertaining to less time requirements. However, the cheetah's fast pace of work can cause the extra time it takes to go back and correct mistakes. The elephant will require more time with a quality piece of work that is well thought out," Erik says then pausing to wince and show deep focused eyes.

"I see these two styles of work each playing a role in our line of work here at Canet. We must first work quick like the cheetah during our prospect calls and work slow and surely like the elephant towards our current buying customers," says Erik.

Roy's eyes widen with his smile while grabbing his chin with his left index finger and thumb saying, "I like being flexible in my line of work, sounds great."

"Oh and Roy, just another perspective with the elephant and cheetah work methods, I believe making three fast paced mistakes is much better than one slow quality mistake. The reason is a mistake or failure is going to be our stepping stone to learn how to succeed." Erik says with a final nod to signal the end of the conversation.

***

Roy is excited the next day when he presents his proposal for three different projects to the Canet Management Team. Coming into the meeting room, there are many ways to improve client sales with seasonal promotions and the right tone of voice. This will spark interest to get approval for the proposal with a majority vote from the Management team.

With the five members of the management team seated in front of a large projector screen, six other employees face them about eight feet away standing with a podium in front of them. The Management Team is made up of three woman and two men, all pass 40 years of age. Unfortunately, the meeting starts off by showing Canet's current revenue and sales for the current year. Roy intends to use the company's current performance as an advantage by using a benefit to cost ratio, proving his proposal will indeed work. With revenue and sales not doing as expected, the fifty plus year old lady in a red suit and brown pulled back hair at the side of the projector screen finally ends her speech by saying, "Ladies and gentlemen, our business has a void. Now, which one of you is going to fill it?"

Roy standing among five others at the podium waits for his turn to present the proposal. Person "A" presents his idea based on selling lights as entertainment features with the Independence Day fireworks lights. The lights will be strung in the air between sky scrapers in cities to enhance the display of colors for people watching fireworks from the ground and on TV. Person "B" presents the idea of selling lights to the National Football League during the Super Bowl Half Time Show. Person "C" proposes selling LED lights to outdoors men and women with a contract with Cabela's Catalog. Person "D" proposes the use of a high watt bulb to be contracted to the U.S. Navy. This high watt light would help submarines and divers see far away while in the water. Person "E" proposes a light that changes color by sliding a multi colored lens underneath the bulb with intentions to sell to sports car manufactures. Person "F" proposes a light with a bulb made of bullet proof glass intended for military and police vehicles. The Management has a lot to choose from and last was Roy's turn.

"Here at Canet, we pride our selves on making and selling quality and efficient lights. My proposal here today is about creating a quality and efficient experience for everyone watching the ball drop on New Years Eve in New York Times Square." Roy says while sweeping his head back and forth to make eye contact with the members of the Management Team in front of him. "I intend to contact the designer of the Times Square New Years Eve Light Show and sell light bulbs like the number of granules in a five pound bag of sugar. Not only for this coming New Year but five New Years into the future, do you know how many lights are purchased and used for the display? Thousands," Roy says while lifting his eye brows with a smile.

"That's not the only subject I will bring up with the City of New York, I'm working on creating a fire cracker that changes colors from a safe non-glass light attached to it," says Roy.

With Roy being the last person to present, the same old lady in the red suit stands up from her seat and walks to the projector screen and says "Impressive ideas, now let the selling begin. All your ideas are sound and backed by a plan of action. The five judges will make the decision on which promotion to go with."

By now it was early afternoon with the sun beaming down bright through the two windows on the east wall. All seven project candidates are seated behind the podiums in a long table facing the judges. As the judges leave in order starting with closest to the door going first, Roy sits nervously waiting for acceptance from the judges to begin the New Year's project. The thought of waiting puts a knot in his stomach and causes him to sweat beads on his forehead. The most significant factor is Roy's most recent sales performance. His good first weeks of work showed promise in his job, but now a rut is occurring. The pressure is on for Roy to get more projects and sales leads to create more business for Canet.

Ten minutes pass by until the judges entered the room with the last judge being the woman in the red suit. She immediately stands when all the judges are seated to announce the decision, "By unanimous decision four to one, Canet will go with the Independence Day Lights and the Bullet Proof Lights for Armored Vehicles. Thanks for everyone's creative ideas, your innovation will create more sales for the future of Canet." With a look of focused eyes the speaker pauses to think of anything more to say and sweeping her face back and forth around the room to keep everyone's attention focused on her. "Details of these two projects with a contact list of leads will be on your desks tomorrow morning. Are there any questions to conclude?" Waiting for a response, she concludes, "Have a great afternoon and let us finish today strong."

With Roy not getting his project chosen from the board, he goes back to the drawing board thinking of new projects to present in future events. His contact list for the remaining leads was not very long as he sat at his cubicle. Recognizing Erik working busily on researching competitor prices, Roy asks, "Erik, have you been accepted to a project by the management team? If so, how did you go about implementing it?"

Erik says, "I have been accepted with doing projects in Hollywood films and fast food franchise projects. I started out by first, constructing the light bulb with our company engineers and second, creating e-mail advertisements featuring the proposed light."

With a new thought, Roy asks, "How about field tests on the lights, and are they done before or after the advertisements are sent?"

"Usually after, Canet will test the light's life duration and durability. Well, I'm going to call it a day. I have a lot of work that needs to wait until morning," says Erik.

Taking his employee badge off the desk next to the computer mouse, Erik heads out into the hallway.

"Have a great day, thanks for the information on proceeding to work after a project has been completed," says Roy.

While receiving a gesturing nod from Erik as he walks kitty corner across the office to the door. Grabbing the door handle with his right hand to pull open the door, he uses momentum generated by the pull and lets his hand go when the door is opened enough to walk out.

CHAPTER 3

Two Months Later

"Where is Roy? He said this new project for Canet would be well worth my time. It's been nearly two months since his last sale, nearly every lead I give him ends up turning to our competitors," says Bob.

Bob is a sales manager at Canet with a long track record of liking sales representatives who are selling and being the drill sergeant for sales boot camp when not selling. As Bob waits in deep thought for an answer from Erik sitting across his desk, each knows the sales have been down, below breaking even for the company budget. Bob has short curly brown hair, a round nose, and a double chin. Easily sixty pounds over weight Bob walks back and forth confidently behind his desks during the conversation with Erik.

Erik says, "Roy is great with designing new projects and viewing the customer's standpoint and purchase power. His ability to create relationships with leads initially needs improvement. In other words, he needs to work towards making a first impression to hook leads. I continue to explain this to him, but I'm afraid much of his efforts are coming from asking for the sale to soon before giving enough time to build a trusting relationship."

While this is being said, Erik cannot look at Bob in the eyes for the fear of finding out in his body language the reality that may happen. Erik looks out Bob's patio window in front of him, behind Bob's desk.

"We have to cut him Erik," Bob says.

The life in Erik's eyes die by being closed shut when hearing Bob. The thought of how to smoothly explain to Roy about the loss of his position at Canet is more than a difficult puzzle to solve, it is a tricky riddle.

"Now there are options for him to remain here at Canet. I have thought about moving Roy to our night shift production line or perhaps doing sales under commission only without hourly pay," Bob says with raised eye brows and a fake smile.

"Well, who is going to break the news to him?" says Erik swallowing to clear his throat.

"I will call him in to inform him after his lunch break. I have a meeting now with Canet's accountant about a realistic budget for the coming months, it seems this company has not been operating within its means," says Bob while picking up his briefcase off the desk and exiting his office.

After lunch break, Erik takes his place in his cubicle to get back to the grind of generating leads, researching companies, and following up with current customers. An hour later, Roy walks in the office cubicle without saying a word and sits down at his desk. In fact, Erik did not notice he was there until there was a "click" on the door latch when the door shut.

"Hey, what is the game plan today?" Erik asks Roy to find out if he has made a decision about his future with Canet.

Roy says, "My game plan today is to work on my current project to convert every potential customer of Canet into a long term customer"

Surprised, Erik says, "Is there anything else new today?

Roy says, "Canet is going to cut my hourly pay and I will continue working with commission. Now, you may not see me as much in the coming weeks at least but all will be back to normal again with a little bit of improvement in my consistency."

"Everyone's sales numbers have dropped, so do not feel inadequate or discouraged. See this as a down streak with success being how far we bounce once we hit rock bottom," Erik says.

"If this is rock bottom, then I feel fortunate to use the momentum of my rapid drop to propel me back to the top," says Roy with a smile on his face for reassurance. There is no sarcasm in Roy's voice and he is confident his sales will pick up soon.

Next, Erik stands up out of his chair, cups his hands together, and shakes them aggressively from cheek to cheek as if he is rolling dice. "Patience my friend, those double six's will show up soon enough," says Erik.

"I hope so," says Roy.

Erik says, 'Don't say "I Hope," say, "I will" because it is going to happen. Just the other day I was reading a book about self talk and the concept of living your vision to the point of talking and acting like it will happen.'

Switching the topic of the conversation, Roy says, "I can work a little more at Chester's Chicken in the evenings. The manager at Chester's would be able to help me out in any pinch that is short term."

Uncertainty filled the room during Roy's speaking to reflect his remembrance of his college days and working extra hours to make it through his last year.

"You are always on top of things, "says Erik.

"I know I will be able to get numerous entry level jobs with my degree," says Roy.

By now, Erik had quietly left, and not wanting to hear Roy's fake role playing with explaining how great his situation is going to build over time. When he looks back a year from now and laughs about how he came through to success.

It is four o'clock in the afternoon and Roy takes a hard look at the road ahead and the impact of his decision making from this point on. Filing away his prospect list and his project for the New Year's Eve proposal, the feet are heavy. Anyone can recognize the additional weight on his shoulders at day's end compared to when he walked in at the beginning of the day. As Roy leaves the office room and walks down the hall way to the elevator, three women pass him all expressing a sad look. This indicates how fast rumors spread about changes with in the company, which is okay with Roy that many people new about his reduction in work. He just shrugs his shoulders and walks on.

"I would have it no other way, for that is my prize for the taking," Roy whispers so none of the three ladies could make out what he was saying as they passed by.

Upon reaching the stairwell at the end of the hall, Roy pushes the door open with a hand placement at shoulder distance apart and at shoulder level. The release of his hands on the door brings his hands together into a clap. The clap position has his hands in a prayer below the chin.

"Let the mayhem begin," Roy says in a deep determined voice.

Roy descends the stairwell swiftly and light on his feet as he says, "goodbye" to everyone he walks past.

***

Business at Chester's Chicken is busier than normal as Roy drives into the parking lot full of vehicles. Roy puts the Chester's Chicken sign on top of his car and walks into the restaurant. The smell of cooked chicken is present from outside of the building.

"Oh, the man of the hour, we have some deliveries for you today. One is at the Main Avenue Park for a birthday party, one at 1385 3rd St. North, and one is at the police station," says Alison the Manager.

Alison is about 5 foot 3" tall with red hair, blue eyes and a freckled face. With even a small movement, her bangs sway back and forth. Not recognizing her small frame is quite possible, with her baggy red shirt hiding her true composition.

"I need to talk about being able to work extra hours when I get back." says Roy.

As he grabs the three delivery bags from the front counter, he tucks one under his arm and grabs one with each hand. The sound of boiling water can be heard in the back kitchen for the broiled chicken. He opens the front door by turning his back to it and pushing it open with his back and walking backwards. The customer bell rings as the door closes behind him.

The day is going to be busy at Chester's due to today being Friday which means most people are out on the town or taking the evening to relax at home. It always seems the same customers will order their customary food item off the menu. The temptation of crispy drummies or baked chicken breast with sauce is too delicious to resist.

Roy now sitting in his car with the deliveries, turns the ignition on with no turn over from the engine. *Oh no, I need this to start, you haven't failed me yet* Trying the ignition again, a large grinding noise starts and quiets down again. *No use, I will have to call a tow truck to get it to the repair shop.*

A half hour later the tow truck comes to tow the car back to the repair shop. In the mean time, Roy is using Alison's car to make deliveries today. The technician at the repair shop explains to Roy over the phone while driving to make deliveries.

"Your transmission in the car is done for and the tires are getting low on tread," says the technician.

A thousand things running through Roy's mind make him tense his shoulders and purse his lips to let out a big exhaled breath. The thought of taking more from his savings account to pay for these car repairs does not help in making deliveries in busy traffic.

"How much do you expect this to cost?" Roy asks in a low tone voice while looking over his shoulder to see if a car is in his blind spot while changing traffic lanes.

"I expect this to come to eight hundred dollars for the transmission and four-fifty if we were to put on new tires," says the repair technician.

Roy says, "How much time do you think it will be until it gets fixed."

"Tomorrow afternoon we should be complete," says the repair technician.

"Ok, go ahead fix the transmission and a new set of tires. I will call tomorrow afternoon to see if it's available" says Roy.

Repair technician says, "We'll make it happen by then, bye."

Hanging up his cell phone, Roy attempts to think of different ways to pay for the car repair. One, pay all twelve hundred fifty dollars with the fifteen hundred dollars in his savings account. Two, pay four hundred dollars with his U.S. savings bonds and eight hundred and fifty dollars with his savings. Three, pay by financing with a loan, thus a person will pay more with interest over the life of the loan.

At Chester's Chicken, deliveries go until midnight and Roy is running on fumes and trying to stay awake with a few cups of coffee.

"What a busy night with over fifty deliveries, that's super bowl business," says Alison, while counting the number of orders.

Showing an open faced smile with eyebrows high and cheeks wide ear to ear, Alison looks over her shoulder at Roy putting the delivery bag in the storage closet next to the oven. The door closet creaks as Roy shuts it with a final push to get it closed.

"Thanks for letting me use your car today to make deliveries Alison. I should be able to get my car fixed by tomorrow's shift," says Roy.

"No problem, those occurrences will happen in this line

of work. Did you want to discuss possible hours available in the coming weeks?" says Alison.

Roy says, "Yes any evening shift would work best."

Alison says, "There are two openings during the holiday on Tuesday and Wednesday."

"Works great, and let me know whenever there is working hours available, as I could use some," says Roy.

***

At the next day's lunch, Roy calls the repair technician from the Canet office phone.

"Steve's Auto Repair," says Steve.

"Yes, I have an eighty-four Lumina in the repair shop getting a new transmission and tires. Will that be ready by this afternoon?" says Roy yawning now due to his early morning rise and walking to work, Roy says, "I can be there between 3:30 and 4:30 today."

Steve says, "Yes, it should be done by then. The total comes to thirteen hundred and thirty dollars with tax."

"I'm on a tight schedule and will be looking to pay for it all up front by check," says Roy.

"Ok, I will have the forms ready when you get here, and have a good rest of your day," says Steve.

"Thanks, you too, bye," says Roy and then hanging up with an expression of anger with eyebrows low and pursed lips.

"Now, all I have to do is call my bank for a transfer" Roy says out loud to himself.

While calling the bank, Roy recognizes Erik talking to Rinae about something that makes them both frown. As Erik and Rinae both stand at the office doorway to the cubicle, both show gestures of concern with raising a straight arm towards Roy.

Roy asks Erik and Rinae, "Is there something going on?"

Just at this point in time, Justin, the lead manager at Canet comes into view at the out side of the doorway.

"Will you have time after your break to come in to my office Roy?" says Justin.

"Yes, I will be right there in a few minutes Justin," says Roy.

Now day dreaming as if he is a deer looking into head lights, Roy thrusts forward out of his chair to stand up. He takes his first step to the office door way as if there are shackles on his feet.

Justin's office is down the hall and to the left up a floor of stairs. The office has the door wide open with Roy entering in and knocking on the door frame. A tick tock sound is coming from a ball and pendulum swinging back and forth on Justin's front desk.

"Roy, have a seat here at my desk. Glad to see you with so short of a notice," says Justin.

"Uh, you should have seen the inquiring interest I had today on the phone line. I'm close to making my next sale," says Roy.

Justin says, "About your sales, I have doubt that you will be able to sell much in coming months. In fact many of our sales reps are cutting little to nothing in the number of sales we generated last quarter. We need to try something different if we are going to stay alive in this business. We have decided to let you go Roy."

Shifting his weight in the chair to cross one leg over the

other, Justin raises his eyebrows with both hands cupped together and holding his top knee up over the bottom knee. Next, switching to a neutral stance again with both feet on the ground, Justin's left hand lifts up to his side with palm facing up and elbow bent as if holding something important. Squeezing the left fist closed, he raises his thin eyebrows once again showing his dark shaded sleepy eyes.

Roy says, "Perhaps I could stay with the company in another department."

"We might have some evening and overnight positions available for clean up and maintenance. Contact HR and ask about any available positions," says Justin.

"Okay, thank you for your time, and I shall be getting on my way," says Roy.

"You are a great individual Roy, our company has to let people go based on seniority," says, Justin.

Getting up out of his chair is a relief for the knot in Roy's stomach. This same knot returns as soon as he leaves Justin's office and has to face the thought of paying bills and looking for work. Back at the office awaits Erik and Rinae, who look at each other upon noticing Roy entering the room. Erik and Rinae both are quiet and waiting for Roy to start with the first words of conversation. Roy remains quiet and checks over his prospect list for the remainder of the day.

After a long minute, Rinae finally says, "I brought some cookies from home. My favorite, monster cookies, please help yourself."

Erik says, "Mmmm, my favorite M&M's."

Roy says, "Just what the doctor ordered to get this knot out of my stomach. I will be leaving after today. Justin told me Canet let me go."

Rinae says, "I'm sorry to hear about that Roy, I don't see

why they would hire someone to a position if they did not have a plan B with what to do if business ever slows down like it is now."

Roy says, "I asked about perhaps being moved to another department, which there might be some spots available. What got to me is the fact that I needed to inquire with HR myself and nothing would be done for me by management with providing options for another job."

Erik says, "I see your point Roy, are you thinking about trying to get into another department with in the company?"

"I will wait and sleep on it for tomorrow. I just have too much on my mind right now," says Roy.

"I will go to HR tomorrow morning and let them know about your credentials and interest in remaining with the company," says Rinae.

"Thanks, Erik and Rinae for your help in sales, I have really come to realize this approach to the feast or famine lifestyle a sales person can endure. I will have to think it over about what I should do next," says Roy.

With a wide grin on his face Erik says, "The tuff times are what makes a person who they truly are."

"Ah, is it for better or for worse?" says Rinae.

Roy says, "It's always for the better, who does it to get worse."

Roy made the last of his calls for the day and managed to add one last buying company to Canet's client list. The smell of fresh print paper will always remind Roy of his first months as a sales representative at Canet Lights.

CHAPTER 4

The next day is not unusual for Roy as it is the start of the weekend. As Monday rolls around, the fact he is without a job hits him. Going to Canet from his apartment building is different with the mind set of trying to get another job there once again.

Upon going through the glass entry way doors, the sound of Mozart music can be heard over the speakers in the entrance lobby.

"Hi, my name is Roy and I was looking to speak with Linda from Human Resources Department," says Roy to the representative at the service desk,

"Yes, I will check to see if she can be right with you." says the representative.

"Okay, no hurry," says Roy.

Upon receiving word by phone the rep says, "Linda will be down to meet you shortly, in the mean time feel free to grab a cup of coffee in the West corner of the lobby."

Roy nods his head to affirm his understanding and walks over to get his usual coffee and cream. After ten minutes, Linda enters the lobby floor and greets Roy with a wide smile having arms behind her back.

Linda says, "Hi my name is Linda, what can I do for you today?"

Roy says, "Yes my name is Roy. I'm looking for an opportunity to find a job here at Canet, what positions are available?"

"Let me get you an application and have it returned with a resume and cover letter as a hard copy or in a fax. Let me give you my card with the fax number info. There are positions that open up quite often," says Linda.

"Ok, I have recently worked for Canet and was terminated due to lack of work. Is there a way I can skip the background check and screening without having to wait?" says Roy.

"We will have to conduct the screening and background check again, it is company policy," says Linda.

Ok, thanks for taking the time to be with me so promptly this morning, as I know you are busy on Monday's," says Roy.

Linda says, "For sure, being a recent employee here will help in the screening process."

Roy stands up out of the lobby chair with his coffee in hand to stand five feet away from the short brown haired Linda. The trickling of water takes away the silence while Linda leaves to retrieve an application for Roy.

"I'll see what I can come up with in a moments notice," says Roy receiving the application from Linda.

The two depart and Roy walks out of the glass entry doors on his way to his car. While reaching into his pocket he notices his keys are not there. Looking into the driver side door, he notices his keys are sitting on the middle compartment coffee holder next to the driver's seat. Being locked out of his car, Roy calls the local tow truck to come open up the car door for twenty-eight dollars.

***

Going back to his apartment, Roy recognizes two police cars parked in the apartment's parking lot. Going into the apartment door, there looks to be as if a bomb went off. All of the drawers and appliances had been pulled out of there respectable places and thrown to the ground. Upon entering his room, the bed was flipped over on its side with no trace of his security case. The case had been taken along with his sports memorabilia collection of Hank Aaron, Walter Payton, and Michael Jordan.

Next, two police officers entered the room and approached Roy.

"My name is Todd Johnson with the Trenton Police Department, is this your apartment sir?" says Todd.

"Yes", says Roy.

"This apartment and another directly above it appears to have been vandalized and robbed," says Todd.

"Yes, they took some of my money, identification papers, and collectables. Damage has been done to my T.V. and computer. Will you be able to find out who did this sir?" says Roy.

"We have no suspects at this moment, but it appears the robber entered through the patio door. We will check the area for finger prints to see what we can find." Todd says.

Roy calls his roommate Nate, and informs him about the robbery at the apartment. Next, he gets a hold of the credit bureau and social security to inform them about his stolen info, which will cost him a hefty fee to get new identification numbers. Roy doesn't have any renters insurance for his items that were stolen and vandalized.

Since the police will be at the apartment through late

afternoon, Roy heads to the public library to search for some job opportunities in the area.

At the library, Roy finds with no surprise that the job market in the area has not changed since last entering the market. With many part time retail and restaurant work, full time truck driver, and factory work listings making up the majority. He goes to print off an application for Canet and a factory job. The first application for Canet prints great, but the following factory application jams the printer causing an irritating screeching noise. Now it's time to make some deliveries.

***

Thankfully, Roy has his delivery job at Chester's Chicken. Upon entering the glass door of Chester's Chicken the place was empty with Alison and another employee at the front cash register sorting out different sizes of beverage cups.

"How are you today Roy?" says Alison with a confident smile on her face.

"Great, today I had my apartment robbed and yesterday I lost my job at Canet," says Roy.

"How do you feel about that?" says Alison.

"I feel like all structure in my life hit the fan," says Roy.

"What do you see as a result of the happenings in the past couple of days and how do you intend to fix it? says Alison.

"I see myself stuck in a deep hole at the bottom of the ocean with a cannon ball chained to my feet. I intend to fix it by starting all over again with nothing at all," says Roy.

"Can you see an opportunity with losing your job and

some of your valuables? What did you learn? Some times tuff experiences make us better and have us utilize inner strength to carry on. Just a way to look at it," says Alison.

Roy shows deep thought with eyebrows high on his forehead. An expression that says thinking that way did not totally occur to him.

"Oh, about you losing some stuff. A person can lose everything they own and still come through to success, all they need is enthusiasm," says Alison.

A few seconds go by and Alison's words finally hook Roy with his eyes widening like a light bulb lighting up.

"Interesting way of making the best of nothing Alison, thanks for the different perspective," says Roy.

"No problem, even though you won't remember it, here is your first delivery of the day," says Alison.

Handing over the counter a hot bucket of chicken, Roy grabs the delivery and puts it in the warming box to carry out to his car. The plastic zipper and Velcro strap of the box encloses all the steam coming from the fresh food.

***

The evening is usual with about four to five deliveries per hour on average. At ten o'clock, Roy is on his last delivery with Chester's closing at around 10:30 PM. Roy is traveling nearby his apartment and at an intersection there is a tall lanky male waiting to walk across the street at the cross walk to his right. The person has a half silver and half black canteen in his hand that looks just like Roy's. The canteen has the colors split down the middle vertically and went missing when his apartment was robbed earlier. The light goes green at the intersection signaling Roy to go, preventing the opportunity to ask the pedestrian where they got the canteen.

Walking up to the top story apartment building, Roy is on time for the delivery and tired from walking up the stairs to the apartment. The delivery goes as usual with the customer leaving three dollars plus extra change without having to break a twenty to even the transaction. On his way down the stairs of the building Roy walks past the same person he seen at the cross walk intersection. The same canteen is present in his hand being silver and black.

"Nice canteen you have there," says Roy.

"Yeah, I got it from a friend," says the mysterious pedestrian.

Looking at Roy's Chester's Chicken Polo shirt, the person turns around and walks away. The person is a tall male in his late twenties with black short hair and a mustache.

The look in Roy's face shows the urge to follow after the mysterious pedestrian, but stalking and confronting about robbing his apartment would not be a safe situation while at work. That silver and black canteen was his father's and is no longer in production.

***

The next day, Roy wakes up to go for a cool morning jog and on his way out the door there is a notice on the front door of his apartment. The notice reads,

"To: Tenant of apartment 122, Roy. The Rent for November is two weeks over due a late fee of seventy five dollars will be charged in addition to your usual rent. If there are any questions or concerns contact me or stop by the front office.

Thanks,

Whirlwind Properties"

The run did not feel very good after receiving a late notice on rent. At around 9 am a phone call comes from Canet.

"Hi, my name is Linda, Human Resources Representative at Canet. I reviewed your application and wanted to inform you about two opportunities during our evening shift. One is a full time production installer and the second is a part time custodial position," says Linda.

"Well, I'm looking for a full time position. What time does the production installer start?" says Roy.

"The shift begins at 11pm and works every other weekend," says Linda.

"That would work with my schedule, I sure would be interested in the position," says Roy.

"I would like to schedule an interview with you to go over some of the duties and requirements for the position. Do you have time tomorrow or Thursday to stop in?" says Linda.

"Tomorrow works, any time before 4pm will work great," says Roy.

"A time at eleven am is open in my schedule, does that work?" says Linda.

"Eleven am works great. Is there any I.D.'s I should bring?" says Roy.

"Your social security card, birth certificate, and a driver's license," says Linda.

"Ok, see you tomorrow," says Roy.

"Bye Roy, I think you will look forward to coming back to Canet," says Linda.

***

The next day at Canet, Roy enters the building hungry for some work. The front lobby is very busy with business executives waiting for appointments and employees heading for lunch. Walking up to the representative at the front counter, she recognizes Roy's face from meeting a few days back.

"Hi, I'm here to see Linda for a job interview," says Roy.

"Yes, one moment sir, I will let her know you are here," says the Representative.

Roy walks over to the waiting lobby just a few feet away to sit on the sofa and try to prepare for the interview questions. In his binder is a copy of his resume and cover letter along with notes on some of his strengths, weakness, and past experience. With other executives waiting next to him, Roy blends in with his white dress shirt and red tie.

"Great to see you here for the interview, I apologize that I'm late. Come with me to my office Roy," says Linda.

"I always like extra time to prepare," says Roy.

The two shake hands and Roy follows Linda up the stairs at the back corner of the lobby.

Roy sit's down in a leather cushioned chair in front of Linda's oak desk. Linda fits the desk perfectly, being five foot nine with her abdomen being level with the desk's work space. Sitting on top of the desk is a clock, pen holder, and a balance sun dial.

"First question I would like to ask, why do you want to work again at Canet?" says Linda.

"Canet is a great place to work due to its people and values of team work, passion, innovation, and customer focus. I like the history of the Company dating back to the 1940's, when the founder Robby Canet, wanted to take advantage of a much needed light bulb product in this country," says Roy.

Linda writes down a summary of what Roy says in her notes and proceeds to asking the next question.

"What are your strengths, and how do you intend to use them at Canet?" says Linda.

"My strengths are the ability to create work by improving methods of productivity. For example, I have come up with a system of e-mailing, calling, and then meeting with prospective buyers in person to sell more products. I used this while selling here at Canet in my previous job. This is my three strikes and you're out method for selling. I know I'm also good at accepting a role on the team and ability to work with other people effectively," says Roy.

"Tell me about your weaknesses?" says Linda.

"My weakness is taking a problem that I'm having to my supervisor or even co-workers. I intend to improve this by asking co-workers what they would do if such and such occurs. I can also tell my supervisor about what I intend to do with a problem and if there are any suggestions available," says Roy.

Linda has written about a half page of notes so far on what Roy has said.

"Tell me about a difficult experience you've had and how you dealt with it?" says Linda.

"Yes, I was ten years old and working on my British Spitfire Airplane Model. One of the last pieces to assemble was the cockpit for the pilot, but there was one problem. It would not fit in the body of the air plane. I remembered the difficulty I had with putting together the body of the air plane in the beginning and decided to trace my steps back to that specific step in the instructions. I found out that I had put one of the T-bars supporting the body together upside down. I adjusted the T-bar and problem solved. Looking back, I pin pointed that one problem related to another and by fixing the initial problem, I was able to fix future problems down the road," says Roy.

"That is a good skill to use on the production line while making our light bulbs," says Linda.

Moving to the next question, Linda looks at her notes in front of her and squints her eyebrows together. As if making a choice about which question to ask next, she makes a mark on her notes and looks up to ask the next question.

"What is your greatest accomplishment?" says Linda.

"My greatest accomplishment is earning my Bachelor's of Science in Marketing as a full time student and working part time. I consider this my defining period to finding what I'm capable of. As I would rather know what my full capacity is compared to not knowing my true potential," says Roy with confidence while looking into Linda's eyes.

"Tell about an experience when you enhanced another person's ability or performance at work," says Linda.

"I worked along side a co-worker and would often complement them on their great ability to find what a customer was looking for in a product we were selling at the time. I helped their process proceed a step further by using a "but" questioning technique to turn every objection that occurs into a positive statement about the fulfillment of what the customer is most interested in. This method greatly improved the number sales for my co-worker," says Roy.

The interview concludes with questions from Roy about hours, benefits, and job advancement, which all are answered by Linda with optimism and not in definite terms. At the end of the interview, the two shake hands and make strong eye contact.

***

The next day, Roy goes shopping for a thank you letter to send to Linda at Canet. Upon leaving the store exit, Roy walks by the same mysterious pedestrian with the canteen; he's reading a classified ad while sitting on a bench. There was no canteen in sight so Roy decides to walk the other direction and not start something he might regret.

Surprisingly, Roy gets a call from Linda at Canet.

"Hi Roy, this is Linda from Canet. I got your thank you letter in the mail and appreciate the time and effort during the interview. In regards to the Production Installer position you applied for, Canet would like to offer you the position," says Linda.

"Yes, I'm very interested after the interview and feel it would be the right fit with my ability to pay attention to detail and multi-task. When can I start?" says Roy.

"Pay period ends this Friday so you can start on Monday at 11 pm," says Linda.

"Great," says Roy.

"Plan to come a half hour early as we have some final paper work for you to complete," says Linda.

"See you then," says Roy.

Hanging up the phone with a smile on his face, then it hits him that his rent needs to be paid. Immediately, the smile leaves his face to a focused game face expression.

Walking over to his room mate's room, Roy notices he is present listening to AC/DC *Hells Bells*.

"Nate, I got a note saying our rent is late this month still. Did you pay your half?" says Roy talking loud to be heard over the music.

Nate is roughly six feet tall with glasses and short brown hair. With a noticeable thick mustache and a United States Marine Corps abbreviation tattooed on his left upper arm, he turns down the music volume.

'Uh, I got canned at my retail job due to a dispute with a customer. It wasn't even my fault. The customer comes in and starts hollering at me about not being able to use a coupon for an item no longer available due to limited quantity. I was like, "If you don't like it go some where else and shop." The manager heard about what I said from the same rude customer and terminated me on the spot for representing the company poorly,' says Nate.

"What are you going to do about the paying your share of the rent?" says Roy.

"I will pay the late fee and my half tomorrow; I had to pay some other bills first. Don't worry, I have a few job applications pending as we speak," says Nate.

"Next time, just let me know if you're going to be late with the rent," says Roy.

"No worries, I do have some savings or extra money's," says Nate.

CHAPTER 5

A few days go by and Monday comes for Roy to clock into his new job at Canet. Leaving a little early from his delivery job, Roy completes the needed paper work with Lisa, an evening supervisor for the production line. Lisa is a brunette in her late forties with brown eyes and long dangling earrings.

"So good to meet you, you must be Roy, my name is Lisa, the production line supervisor," says Lisa.

"Yes, I have arrived early to complete paper work before my shift starts," says Roy.

"Take a seat in the lobby chair, here are the forms and if you have any questions be sure to let me know," says Lisa.

"Thanks, I've done this before, so there shouldn't be a problem," says Roy.

"Also, this is Ben, he will be training you into your position for the first few days," says Lisa.

Next to Lisa stands Ben, a long haired man wearing safety glasses in his late twenties.

"Hi Roy, ready to hit it hard today?" says Ben.

"Oh do go easy on him for the first day," says Lisa with a concerned expression.

"No worries, I'm sure Roy will catch on quick," says Ben.

Roy goes over to the lobby chair completes the paper work and hands it to Lisa in time for the start of the shift.

"Roy with this job, do start with the end in mind," says Lisa.

Ben and Roy walk through the employee double doors to the production line consisting of four lines marked A, B, C, and D.

'When she said start with the end in mind" is she talking about the end of the shift?' says Roy talking to Ben as they walk.

"Roy, we will be on the B line mostly, which makes the specialty lights such as Christmas lights, neon signs, and strobe lights. When coming to work, punch into your work line computer using your employee ID number," says Ben.

The station looks as if a tornado went through it with the computer not on and papers strewn all over the counter top. Ear plugs are a must on the production line with the loud factory machines running. This makes it a must to talk loud to anyone that you are speaking to.

"Your job today is to install the extension cords for the neon signs and strobe lights. Use the Philips Screw Driver to tighten the electrical wires to the chip receiver in each neon sign," says Ben.

With a neon sign on the belt spaced out about every five feet, there are control buttons to stop and start the belt so a person can work on the signs without moving around a lot. A supply cart on wheels holds all the tools and extension cords to be installed. While there are a lot of production line workers around, none of them are within twenty feet of Roy.

"The location to screw the wire into is here," says Ben

pointing to the bottom of the sign where the electric chip is located.

"The next step is to take this cover, place it over the chip, and snap it into place. Then the sign is flipped on the conveyor belt front side up so that you can read it for the next person to start their task," says Ben.

"So there are three different steps, one- install the plug-in cord, two- install the cover, and three- flip it front side up," says Roy.

"Correct, I think you can handle it," says Ben with a smile on his face.

***

Back at home, Nate is been putting in some applications when Roy walks into the apartment around 7:30 am.

"How was the first day," says Nate working on his computer.

"Great, I found out that with doing the same thing over and over a person gets the hang of it on the twelfth time," says Roy.

"How do you even keep count?" says Nate.

Roy smiles and nods at the question. Roy has been noticing Nate at the apartment more than usual after losing his job.

"Nate, how is the job search coming, and did the rent get paid?" says Roy.

"I have it covered and one job interview is scheduled for tomorrow. I will pay rent tomorrow," says Nate.

"Ok, if you need help let me know. Let's keep our standing with the landlord in good terms," says Roy entering his room to fall asleep and shutting the door behind him.

Nate continues to work diligently on his applications when his cell phone rings.

"Well, when will you be moving in?" says the caller on the other line.

"The quickest way I will get out is being evicted. Tony, it will be a few weeks at the earliest," says Nate.

"Your rent will be much cheaper here, the neighbor across the hall works at the food shelf and gives out free non-perishable food items every month," says Tony.

"Talk about a money saver that will be," says Nate.

"That's not the only connection I have, my uncle owns the Cenex station on 8th ave, we're talking about free gas," says Tony giving Nate a surprising look on his face.

***

A few weeks later, Roy wakes up in the afternoon and goes to his car to grab his cell phone. Upon opening the door to the apartment, an envelope drops to the floor from the door frame. The letter reads, "A NOTICE OF EVICTION" Roy opens the envelope quickly.

"The rent for the month of November and December is past overdue and company policy states, with two consecutive months in of incomplete rent payments instills an eviction from the apartment. You will have three days to gather belongings, which will be confiscated if not removed by December 11th, 2001."

No longer reading the letter, Roy walks to Nate's room and knocks on the door and abruptly opens the door not waiting for a response. Nate is sitting at his desk and listening to some music playing on a CD player.

"Roy, I have the coolest idea with impressing the person interviewing me today," says Nate.

"I received a notice of eviction for this apartment from our landlord. Next time, let me know when your half of the rent is not being paid so I can get it paid," says Roy.

"Oh my bad, I'm sorry Roy. Do you think we can try talking to the landlord about staying? I have been kind of tight with money and have other debt that I have been paying off," says Nate.

"Well, do you want to go half and half for paying for a U-haul to get our stuff out of here?" says Roy.

"Yes, I need some of my furniture moved. Where do you plan on moving to?" says Nate.

"I will probably move closer to Canet on the south side of town. My brother has an apartment there, so I will probably move in with him," says Roy.

"Yeah, I will be at my friend Tony's about a few blocks away, until I find a permanent place to live, says Nate.

"Nate lied to me, he knew about the rent when I asked him about it a few weeks ago. He didn't pay the rent because he wants out now without having to wait for the three month notice to vacate. I should have questioned him more to figure out what he was up to, now my line of credit is worse," whispers Roy to himself.

"Well, we have a few days to get out and get this place cleaned up. Is there time today or tomorrow to get the process started?" says Roy.

"Yeah, I will get some boxes from the local grocery store and start packing everything up. Oh, I have an idea to shoot for. Let's pack everything up today, move everything out tomorrow, and clean the day after tomorrow," says Nate.

"Great idea, I will roll with that," says Roy.

With the boxes and everything packed by that afternoon, Roy heads to his delivery job. Not many deliveries are taking place on a weekday like this. This is a time to fold delivery boxes, restock sales receipts, and hand out the "Buy five and get one Chester's Chicken Free" coupons.

"What coupon special are you going to run for the holiday season," says Roy.

"The buy a six piece chicken wing basket and get second half off comes to mind," says Alison.

"Great idea, how exactly does that work for mark up and profitability?" says Roy.

"Of course, we have to increase the mark up of a six piece wing basket to almost fifty percent so that we break even with providing the customer with two baskets. Where we are looking to make money is in the drink," says Alison.

"The drink…. huh," says Roy.

"Most people will want something to drink or an appetizer with their chicken and the coupon does not include the drink. When the drink is purchased, the mark up or profit is made with that item," says Alison.

"I see, it's still a great deal though," says Roy.

"A person will probably save three to four dollars on the chicken," says Alison.

***

Roy and Nate help each other the next day to move everything out of the apartment and by the third day the cleaning commences.

"Are you sure you know what the landlord will be looking

for when going over the cleanliness of the apartment?" says Roy.

"Yeah, I have done this before," says Nate.

"I called the carpet cleaner yesterday and they will be by today at 3:30. What do you say? Go fifty fifty split with the cleaning bill?" says Roy.

"Yeah, that sounds even," says Nate.

"I never realized the oven was this dirty," says Roy, cleaning the inside of the oven with oven cleaner.

"Well there was that time your home made hot dish burnt and flooded the apartment in smoke," says Nate.

"Yeah, I forgot to put on the timer while doing my laundry," says Roy.

"Wasn't the dish ruined because the burnt food melted into the dish?" says Nate.

"Yeah that was one of my new dishes too," Roy says with a laugh.

"Well, I have to go to work and will meet you here tomorrow at two to do a final walk through with the landlord," says Roy.

"Yeah, hopefully we get most of our deposit back," says Nate.

Chapter 6

"Well, what do you expect? The reason why we got only two thirds of our deposit is because a landlord always tries to make money off of a tenant one way or another when they move out." says Roy, talking on the telephone to Nate.

"Yeah, I guess I will run into you later Roy, take care," says Nate on the other line.

"You too," says Roy.

Hanging up the phone, Roy's brother James walks into the living room and faces Roy who is seated slouching in the recliner.

"Before you get settled in, Tom and I have some ground rules established that everyone must follow. One, if you're listening to music past ten pm, use head phones. Two, if you anticipate being late on paying your third of the rent, let us know so that we can pay it and that same person late for rent will pay for an entire month's worth of groceries. Three, if a girl friend is here more than four out of seven days a week, the two of them need to find another place to wazzle and dazzle," says James.

"Got it bro, no need to worry I have never been late with the rent, don't have a music player, and no girl friend," says Roy.

"That's the case so far, wait until temptation hits head

on. Yeah well, the real world is a tough place, but if you expect it to be tuff, a person will be prepared and better able to get back up once they have fallen down," says James.

"I can see from the USMC tattoo on your left shoulder in relation to what you just said," says Roy.

"This must be James's bro, how are you? My name is Tom," says Tom. With his heavy weight frame, Tom holds out his right hand for a hand shake while standing next to James. During the hand shake, a nice silver Rolex wrist watch catches Roy's attention.

"Nice watch," says Roy.

"You have no idea what I went through to get it," says Tom.

"I believe you," says Roy.

"This is a three bedroom apartment costing twelve hundred dollars a month, Roy. Do you think there will be problems paying the four hundred and a twenty-five dollar share for the electric bill?" says James.

"I do not think there will be a problem," says Roy.

Roy walks over to the door and grabs hold of the cold brass door knob.

"Where are you going Roy?" says Tom.

"I'm heading to the store, need anything?" says Roy looking over his right shoulder at Tom seated in a chair.

"No, adios amigo," says Tom.

***

At the grocery store, Roy waits in line at the customer service desk. With beeping sounds coming from the check out lanes behind Roy, time seems to slow down like watching the second hand on a clock, he finally gets his turn.

"Hi, my name is Roy, and I'm looking to see if you are currently hiring," says Roy to the women at the customer service desk.

"Yes, here is an application and our job postings are usually posted on the bulletin board in the exit doors," says the customer rep while pointing over to exit to her left.

"Thank you for your time," says Roy grabbing the application.

Walking over to the exit bulletin board, Roy see's there is a cake decorator from the bakery and a night shift cashier available.

"Ah, I need a day shift before four in the afternoon," says Roy quietly to himself. Going back to the apartment, Roy walks a mile in the cool December weather.

Roy fills in the application writing, *Day shift (any position)* in the position applying for section of the form. The section listing skills Roy writes, *experience working with customers of light fixtures, processing customer orders, explaining the benefits in the sales process, and being dedicated to making deliveries on time with products.*

Walking back into the same grocery store moments later, Roy is in his white dress shirt and red tie to turn in the job application to a different customer service rep this time.

"Hi, my name is Roy and I have a job application to turn in," says Roy.

"Sure, I will put this into the manager's files," says the women at the customer service counter.

"Thank you for your time," says Roy.

***

The next day, Roy just about falls asleep around nine in the morning when his cell phone starts to ring. Raising his head off of the pillow and reaching for the cell phone sitting on a night stand, Roy answers.

"This is Roy," says Roy with an irritated voice upon waking up from a resting state.

"Hi Roy, my name is Sherry, with Harry's Food Market. I'm calling about your application I have," says Sherry.

"Yes, I'm looking for a shift during the day," says Roy.

"I can see that from your application, we do have a stocker position available starting at eight and ending at three thirty. Responsibilities include stocking sales items on the shelf, counting inventory, and building and taking down displays," says Sherry.

"The Stocker position sounds interesting and the right fit for me," says Roy.

"Is there a time you can come in for an interview on Wednesday or Thursday of this week?" says Sherry.

"Yes, Thursday works at 11:30 am," says Roy.

"Sounds great I will see you then, bring two forms of identification also," says Sherry.

"Okay, bye," says Roy.

Hanging up the phone, Roy plops his face back onto his pillow and wakes up at 2:30 in the afternoon. Heading out the door of his room, Roy sees Tom sitting on the living room sofa reading a book.

"Hey Tom, how is it going?" says Roy.

"Great, I had today off and thought I would catch an interesting read," says Tom while looking over his shoulder to Roy who is standing in the kitchen area.

After preparing his peanut butter and jelly sandwich,

which Roy devours in an instant, Roy continues the conversation.

"I have a job interview with Harry's Food Market," says Roy.

"Yeah, do you think you can handle a third job Roy?" says Tom putting his book away.

"It'll just be part time. Besides, I'm looking for ten to fifteen hours more each week," says Roy.

"I've done it before, one of the toughest things I ever did," says Tom.

"Is that how you paid for that nice silver Rolex?" says Roy.

"I used an investment of a lot of time and Vivarin to obtain my Rolex," says Tom.

"I'm aware of the concept of time, but never heard of Vivarin," says Roy.

"It's a caffeine pill that I used to extend my time," says Tom.

With a squinting look in his eyes, Roy thinks about what Tom did to get to where he is today. Tom basically worked sleep deprived, slept, and ate.

"Sounds to me like burn out," says Roy.

"You do it long enough and a person gets used to it. What do you think it's going to be like with this third job now?" says Tom.

"I'm sure I can handle it. There are no jobs right now relating to my degree and if there are, it's part-time without any benefits," says Roy.

"Either way we must pick our poison," says Tom.

"What poison?" says Roy.

"The poison of the picking of the litter, the first pick of

the litter is destined for greatness, the last pick of the litter is the under dog. The dog which must work twice as hard as everyone else to get where they want to go," says Tom.

"Were you the underdog, Tom?" says Roy.

"I was the underdog at the bottom of the Grand Canyon," says Tom.

***

The next day, Roy get's two and a half hours of sleep and wakes up in time for his job interview. He gets showered and dressed up to make it in time for his 11 am appointment at the grocery store.

"Hello, how are you today sir?" says Sherry, a short brunette with a tan colored shirt and "Harry's Foods" embroidered on the front.

"Great, ready to dive into the stocking position you have here at Harry's Foods." says Roy.

"I'm sure the person will have their hands full. Come on over to my office in the back of the store," says Sherry pointing to the far northeast corner of the store.

Upon entering through the wooden door of Sherry's office, Roy sits down in one of the two leather swivel chairs in front of her desk.

"Roy, first tell me about your past work experience and how the experience will qualify you for the stocking position here at Harry's Foods," says Sherry.

"I have worked at Chester's Chicken as a delivery driver which requires attention to time and communication with customers. Both time and communication are a skill that I can see utilized at the stocking position here. I also work at

Canet Lights on the production line, which requires great attention to detail," says Roy.

"Very correct, both are important. What do you consider your greatest weakness and how do you intend on handling it here at our store?" says Sherry.

"I consider my greatest weakness to be finding different products that customers are looking for in the store. I will handle this weakness by becoming aware of where products are located with the repetition of daily stocking tasks and asking a co-worker where a product is located," says Roy.

"Explain when you experienced a conflict in work place and how you handled it?" says Sherry.

"A conflict that I experienced in the work place is when a customer at Chester's Chicken was mad at me when I arrived late for his delivery. I explained my situation with bad traffic and many deliveries. A reaffirming free chicken basket and an apology was also issued by me. I was also able to keep my emotions under control during the time the customer was rude to me," says Roy.

"I would say you handled the conflict the best you could with what the situation was like. Do you have any problems working in cooler environments such as the cooler and freezer in the back?" says Sherry.

"No, I do not know of any reason right now that might be a problem for me," says Roy.

"The position calls for eight am to three thirty for two days a week, Friday and Sunday specifically. Will these days and times work for your schedule?" says Sherry.

"Sure will," says Roy.

The interview continued with Sherry asking questions

and Roy answering with good eye contact and straight forward, honest answers.

***

"Well bro how did you do?" says James while at the apartment.

"I think I did well, but you know there is always room for improvement," says Roy.

"Do you really need this third job, Roy," says James.

"Yes, I'm tired of going from pay check to pay check with little left over. Besides, it's a natural human characteristic to want more and I know I deserve more money than I make right now," says Roy.

"I know all about it, the year before I joined the Marines was tough making minimum wage," says James.

"This will be a good challenge for me to test what I can and cannot do, what my true limits are," says Roy.

"There is nothing wrong with finding your limits by reaching for a threshold. You will find that you can do more than you think. If you need any help, be sure to ask," says James.

"I'm sure there will be no worries," says Roy.

***

The next day, Roy gets a phone call again waking him up this time at one thirty in the afternoon.

"This is Roy," says Roy.

"Hi Roy, this is Sherry calling from Harry's Foods. How are you today?" says Sherry.

"Great and you?" says Roy.

"I'm doing great, we would like to offer you the stocker position," says Sherry.

"Great, I'm interested in the position and it would work great with my schedule," says Roy.

"Welcome to the team, when can you start?" says Sherry.

"Next Friday is a good start," says Roy.

"Okay stop in some time during the day before next Friday and we can get some final paper work done for you to start. As of right now, you will start at eight in the morning next Friday," says Sherry.

"Okay, talk to you later and have a great day," says Roy.

Roy hangs up the phone and decides that he might as well get up because once he falls asleep; he will just need to get up again any way.

***

As next Friday comes closer and closer, Roy mentions to Tom his schedule with the new job starting.

"Monday, I work eleven to seven thirty at Canet; Tuesday eleven to seven thirty at Canet and four to ten thirty at Chester's," says Roy with an interruption from Tom.

"Now is the Monday shift at Canet fall under the category of Sunday night into Monday or Monday night into Tuesday because I'm confused about which day?" says Tom.

"The Monday night into Tuesday is considered a Monday shift, which is quite nice. Wednesday is the Canet hours, Thursday just Canet on the night shift; Friday, Harry's Food's from eight am to three thirty, Chester's, and then

Canet to follow. Saturday morning I have off until Chester's four to ten thirty, Canet eleven to seven thirty; Sunday, Harry's eight to three thirty" says Roy.

"So Roy, you work every other weekend at Canet and will have to stay awake from Thursday afternoon into Saturday morning on those weekends," says Tom.

"Yes, Saturday morning I will get some time to sleep each week and I have Chester's Chicken Saturday evening, Canet to follow, and then Harry's Food's Sunday. The good news is I have from Sunday afternoon to Monday evening off to recuperate for the next week," says Roy.

"Yep, either energy drinks or caffeine will be your crutch to get you through the weekend. That is a total of forty plus eighteen plus fourteen totals to be seventy two hours a week, almost two full time jobs," says Tom.

***

The Friday morning after leaving work at Canet, Roy is tired as he has been working for more than eight hours. The drive to Harry's Foods' is quicker than thought as it only takes Roy ten minutes to drive from Canet to the grocer. Roy quickly changes his t-shirt into the Harry's tan polo in the restroom of the store.

"Hi Roy," says Sherry standing at the front of the store with a gentleman who's been in directly talking to her face to face.

"Hi Sherry," says Roy.

"This is Sally, she will be walking you through your job description today," says Sherry directing eye contact from Roy to Sally.

"Nice to meet you Sally," says Roy.

"And it's nice to meet you too," says Sally a brunette about a few inches taller than Roy.

"If you have any questions Roy, call the supervisor on duty at 381," says Sherry.

"First we will go to the back of the store to show the mess we get to organize and stock at each shift, come with me," says Sally.

Walking to the back of the store where the swinging doors enter into the back room, Sally points to her left at one of the product displays at the end of the aisle.

"Later today, we will be changing that display to next week's cereal item that is on sale," says Sally.

Walking through the swinging doors, the back room has three levels of racking to hold pallets of product inventory. Sally comes to a stop by the receiving doors kitty corner to Sherry's office where Roy interviewed for the position.

"These three pallets of product are newly received and need to be organized onto the u-boat carts and filled to the shelf on the sales floor," says Sally.

"Okay, is there a convenient way to recognize where an item goes to?" says Roy.

"Yes, Roy there is an item number on the case of each product that is the same number on the shelf tag. A lot of knowing where something goes is through trial and error with repetitively being on the sales floor more and more often. Later, we will have to fill the sales item this week to the shelf. All of the sales items are located on that racking to our left by the coolers," says Sally.

"Well, let's get started and get the feet wet," says Roy.

"That's the spirit," says Sally.

Picking up the first item and putting it onto cart one

of five, Roy starts organizing the messed up pallets. Most of Roy's shift is spent organizing product pallets, stocking product to the shelf, assisting customers to help find what they are looking for, and changing the one cereal display. By the time three thirty rolls around, Roy clocks out and heads directly to his car for Chester's Chicken. Having bought an energy drink on his brake, Roy engulfs the drink on his way over to Chester's for what will be a busy Saturday night.

"Hey Roy, how is the new job going for you?" says Alison.

"Uh, the one at Canet?" says Roy.

"Yes, didn't you get on the night shift in the production line?" says Alison.

"Sure did, it's adequate and wonderful that I'm always on my feet to stay awake,'" says Roy.

"If that is adequate, then what is this job?" says Alison folding Chicken boxes.

"An opportunity in disguise," says Roy.

"I have four deliveries for you right now, which shouldn't take long, as they are close by," says Alison.

Roy gets through his Friday Chester's shift and heads over to Canet very sleepy and tired. On the production line, Roy takes a caffeine pill to stay awake. Time fly's by and Roy gets to his car while running on fumes and caffeine jitters. Dragging his feet, finally Roy gets his head to the pillow. He sets his alarm clock for three in the afternoon for Chester's evening shift.

CHAPTER 7

"Hello this is Canet Lights, how can I help you?" says the Canet Representative on the phone.

"Hhhhi, this is Roy Monte and I'm sick today and will not be making it in for the shift today," says Roy with a tired and ill voice.

"Okay, thanks for calling in and get well soon," says the rep.

"Hello, it's a wonderful day at Harry's Foods this is Stacy," says Stacy at Harry's Foods.

"This is Roy Monte calling about not being into work today, I'm sick and too ill to perform my duties," says Roy.

"Yep, we will look for you to come in on Sunday," says Stacy.

"Welcome to Chester's Chicken, this is Alison," says Alison.

"Hi Alison, cannot make it in for today's delivery shift due to being ill," says Roy.

"Okay, if you say so, is everything going well?" says Alison.

"Yes, I need to get over this fever and get some rest," says Roy.

"Get well soon Roy," says Alison.

After hanging up the phone, Roy goes back to sleep

and does not wake until ten hours later, which is nine in the evening. Getting up to go to the kitchen, Roy gets something to drink. The fridge light turns on and provides a back shadow on Roy with all the lights being turned off in the kitchen. Tom and James are sitting on the couch in the living room watching T.V.

"Aren't you supposed to be at work?" says Tom.

"Yes, I called in sick due to not feeling good," says Roy.

"That flu is going around you know," says James.

"I heard a quick way to kill a cold is to fast. Do you think the same can be said for the flu?" says Tom.

"Well, I don't feel like eating a thing, should I try?" says Roy.

"Make sure you drink plenty of water, Roy," says James.

"I'm filling up a water bottle as we speak," says Roy.

***

Two Days Later…

"Two days it's been since Roy has had this illness. Should we take him to the doc?" says Tom.

"I'll go check on him," says James going across the living room into Roy's room.

"That is a bad idea. Last time I went into his room while he was sleeping, he started going crazy in his sleep," says Tom.

"How's it going Roy?" says James.

"Still cold and running a fever, will you go and check

on my car? It's been a couple of days since operating it," says Roy.

"Sure, I will be right back," says James leaving the room to go check on the car.

A few minutes later, James comes back into the apartment building and enters Roy's room who is half awake.

"Roy buddy, I've got some news. The car has been vandalized with its windshield broken and electrical wiring cut out of the hood and dashboard," says James.

"What? No way," says Roy with eyes wide to show their redness.

"This must have occurred last night because I came home after work yesterday and your car looked fine from what I could see," says James.

"I've missed three days of work and will miss even more with this being done to my car," says Roy.

"Sorry bro, but I will not be able to lend you a car during your delivery job, I need a car for my job as well," says James.

"I will just ride the bus to work, it is only a few miles at the most," says Roy.

"What will you do at night for the delivery job?" says James.

"I will go back to work tomorrow if I feel better. I will tell my supervisors that due to car trouble, I may be running a little late," says Roy.

"Ok, if they are fine with that, I would be surprised," says James.

***

The next day is Wednesday and Roy has been gone from

work since Friday. Roy only has Chester's and Canet to go to for work.

"This is Canet Lights, how can I make your world brighter?" says the representative on the phone.

"Hi, my name is Roy Monte and will be running late for work today," says Roy.

"Ah, thank you for letting us know," says the Canet Rep.

Things did not go as smooth with Alison at Chester's.

"Hi Roy, are you feeling better?" says Alison upon picking up the phone.

"Yeah, feeling better, listen I will be running a little late on Friday because I'm without a car," says Roy.

"Wow, my car is not available too, so I do not have anything to lend you this time," says Alison.

"I brought my car to a repair shop to see what they can do to fix it" says Roy.

"I need you to have a reliable car Roy, this is the second time this month there has been no car," says Alison.

"Well, the car was vandalized this time around," says Roy.

"I've seen you at Harry's Foods the other day working Roy. Do you work three jobs right now?" says Alison.

"Yeah, I work at Harry's as well as Canet," says Roy.

"That's too much Roy, I have decided to have you work Friday and Saturday deliveries only," says Alison.

"Ok, what should I do today with no car?" says Roy.

"I will have my uncle in for delivery, you mean while, can have the evening off," says Alison.

"Ok, I should see you on Friday," says Roy trying to

end the phone conversation to avoid expressing his anger of missing more work hours.

"Let me know of the status of your car by Thursday. I have to go, bye" says Alison hanging up the phone.

At the apartment with James and Tom lazily reclining on the sofa, Roy looks at his calendar for the upcoming week.

"I have between an hour to thirty minutes going from one job to the next each day. When I have an hour between jobs, I will walk and with a half hour I will ride the bus," says Roy.

"Well, the time schedule is about the same, right. The distance from Canet to Harry's is closer than the distance from Harry's to Chester's Chicken," says James.

"That is a good point I can easily walk from Canet to Harry's and just take the bus from Harry's to Chester's Chicken. I do believe the bus will take me that direction," says Roy.

"If you need a ride, just let me know because I get off from work at 3:30 in the afternoon," says Tom.

"Ok, that'll do," says Roy.

Next, Roy's phone rings.

"Hi Roy," says the lady on the other line.

"Yeah," says Roy.

"This is Marla with your car at the repair shop. We looked into getting an estimate of what it will take to fix your car. The total repairs come to nine hundred and thirty with the new windshield and wiring and sixty dollars for the tow," says Marla.

"Okay, is it ready right now or when do you think it will be available?" says Roy.

"Yeah, we're quite busy right now so it will be done for sure by Friday. Would you like us to call you when it is ready?" says Marla.

"Yes, that would be greatly appreciated," says Roy.

"Okay, you have a great day," says Marla.

"Bye, Marla," says Roy hanging up the phone.

"Now I have to come up with over a grand to get my car fixed," says Roy.

"Will you have trouble making the rent payment pal?" says James.

"I should be fine man, keeping the enthusiasm is most important right now. I've run close to being in debt, but not this close before. I'm so frugal right now that I do not want to eat. I'll see how far I will bounce when I hit rock bottom," says Roy.

"Well, don't get one of those pay day loans. I tried doing that once and it came back to haunt me. Even though I had gotten enough money initially, the next month I had to pay the same bill and the payday loan with interest. I had a deeper hole to dig myself out of," says Tom.

"I have over a few hundred dollars left, which should become a last resort at all costs," says Roy.

"You definitely should be having some extra money coming with working three jobs. As long as a person lives below their means in this way, they should be doing fine," says Tom.

Standing up to walk out the door, Roy says, "I get to head out to the bus stop."

"Good luck at Canet this evening Roy," says James.

The evening air is cold with a bite as Roy walks the two blocks to the bus stop; the air is cold enough to have his exhaled breath visible. With the accompanying traffic busily driving by next to the side walk, Roy goes through the motions of placing one foot in front of the other to carry him along as he day dreams of owning his own business some day.

"My current reality is a situation of extreme difficulty, a situation of everyone taking advantage of the little man. Well, what if in the end I achieve everything I set out to accomplish with focus and perseverance," says Roy to himself.

Crossing the street intersection at a stop light is very uneasy for Roy. A driver does not come to a complete stop soon enough and enters the vehicle into the cross walk almost hitting Roy. Roy side steps a few feet to avoid being hit by the car. Walking the next block, Roy is in the fight adrenaline response. His face burns with the strong bite of the wind. Upon hocking a loogy to the ground, the moisture seems to freeze instantly upon leaving his mouth.

'Every once in a while, I will be at work and have a customer or co-worker tell me, "have faith" or "I will see you next week, if you are still here." What do they see when they look into my eyes. My situation is not so bad. I guess I would rather not have it any other way,' says Roy talking to himself again.

Entering the warm bus is a pleasant relief for Roy. Surprisingly, Roy notices the same tall person with his canteen sitting in the second front seat of the bus. The only seat remaining open is the third front row seat. Roy sits down and contemplates whether opening up a conversation with the person having what looked to be his canteen.

"How's it going, you are the chicken man making

deliveries, right?" says the mysterious person sitting in front of Roy in the second row.

"Yes, my name is Roy, what is your name?" says Roy.

"My name is Benny, I must live close to you because I usually see you around a lot," says Benny.

"Yeah, I actually just moved to the south side of town. The canteen you have there, where did you get it?" says Roy.

"I got it at the local pawn shop just a few weeks ago," says Benny.

"Huh, that canteen looks very familiar to the one that was taken from me almost a month ago," says Roy.

"Well, I paid fifteen dollars for it, you can have it for that," says Benny with a wide smile and making his mustache widen.

"No thanks, I did not have any use for it as it is considered a collectable," says Roy.

The rest of the bus ride goes by very quick. The bus gets to a stop one hundred yards from the Canet Light building. Getting off is a very unpleasant experience as the cold rushes its strong wind. Looking down the road to the one hundred yard stretch, the best bet is to take distance in increments of four street lights at a time. Taking the least common denominator and proceeding the cold walk one street light's distance at a time.

"Hi, how are you Roy?" says Linda while leaving out the front door of the building with Roy holding the door open for her.

"Great, I'm feeling much better now," says Roy.

It's always on my mind, having only a few hundred dollars in my bank account. Any slip now and I can have a real mess on my hands. My first paycheck comes tomorrow and we will see if I get all my bills paid. Right now, less is more." says Roy to himself.

The first half of Roy's shift goes by slow with his tight finances in the back of his mind. Then comes the unexpected at the end of his shift for the day.

"Hey Roy this is Al at the Auto Repair. Uh, regarding your car the costs come to be about eleven hundred dollars with our windshield warranty," says Al.

"Do you have any financing options consisting of a monthly payment?" says Roy.

"Yeah, we have a provider at Stewart featuring zero interest for the first six months. I can get working on the car today for an estimated finish time of at least 48 hours," says Al.

"Now is the time to get started, I will call back in a couple of days, bye," says Roy, hanging up the phone.

Walking to Harry's Foods is an up hill battle as it turns out to be a cold morning with lots of wind and snow. Walking along the side walk with oncoming forty mile per hour traffic makes the wind rush in waves as multiple cars pass by in the morning rush hour.

"Ah, the rule of half and half, I have two options. Why not split my money equally with the number of options that I have. It would not be smart to put my remaining three hundred dollars in the auto repair payment and I should put some type of down payment for the repair," says Roy to himself while waiting for the cross walk signal to turn green.

The cross walk signal turns green to walk across the walk way to the other side of the street; this is a magnificent sight with all three car lanes being filled up and vehicles stopping up parallel to the cross walk line on the street.

Suddenly, Roy falls on the pavement tripping from a pothole. Face planting into the pavement, Roy gasps for breath in order to alleviate the sudden adrenaline rush occurring. Rising to his hands and knees, Roy brings his fingers to his front tooth to recognize that it is chipped.

"Are you all right man?" says a driver of a car stopped right behind the crosswalk next to Roy.

"Yeah, I'll live to see another day," says Roy still on his hands and knees.

"Great, now can you get up so I can get to work on time?" says the driver.

"Oh, didn't mean to hold you up," says Roy.

***

At Harry's Foods, Roy enters into the break room and walks by Stacy, a customer service employee in her late thirties with brown hair.

"What happened to you? There is blood on your lip," says Stacy.

"I fell on the pavement on the way to work this morning and chipped my tooth," says Roy.

Going directly into the restroom to see his face in the mirror, Roy recognizes blood running down from his lower lip. Smiling wide, Roy recognizes his left front tooth chipped off half way. Wiping the blood off his face with a paper towel, Roy suddenly shifts his focus to the black circles under his eyes. The long working days have taken its toll with a counter balance of knowing everything will turn out just fine.

"I'm doing everything possible to get through this mess, as long as I keep trying things will be just fine," says Roy to himself looking in the mirror with a depressed look on his face.

By the time the shift ends at Harry's Foods, Roy begins the journey back home to rest. The weather outside is still cold with ice on the roads from the day's snow fall. Being bundled up head to toe helps to endure the cold wind chill, but its not just the cold, the ice makes a person penguin walk also.

"Believe," says Roy to himself walking into his apartment building.

***

"This is Dr. Thompson's office. How can I help you? Jane speaking," says Jane, a customer representative at the dentist's office.

"Yes, I have a chipped tooth that needs to be fixed, it's the front tooth of my top jaw," says Roy.

"What is your name sir and what days can you make it in?" says Jane.

"My name is Roy and the thing is I work three jobs and can make it in only on Monday or Tuesday afternoons," says Roy.

"Well we do have an opening at four in the afternoon on Monday. Does that work?" says Jane.

"Yes it works great, schedule me for that time," says Roy.

"We will see you Monday at four pm, bye," says Jane.

"Yes, thank you," says Roy.

***

Saturday, Roy gets his car back in the evening with a ride from his brother.

"Does the Stewart Financing option work for you today?" says Al.

"Yes, I have one hundred and fifty dollars to put down today and would like to loan finance the remainder," says Roy.

"Works great, we can do a six or twelve month finance option. The six month has a payment of $216 per month, the twelve month has a payment of $108 per month," says Al with eyebrows high and to make his forehead wrinkle and eyes fixed on his computer screen.

"Think about the money you will be saving by going with the six month plan," says James whispering to Roy.

"I'll go with the six month plan," says Roy.

"The six month plan it is, here is the form in which we need a bank account on file for any default periods," says Al sliding the form across the desk to Roy standing next to James.

After completing all two pages and reading the terms and conditions entirely, Roy exchanges the form for his car keys.

"Okay, I will bring in my payment next month," says Roy.

"Sounds good, let us know if you will be late on the payment ahead of time. We can try to work with you if you work with us," says Al.

Starting the car, Roy's heart felt like it grew twice its size with the relief of having his car back.

"Yes, now let's get some sleep," says Roy to himself with extreme enthusiasm.

***

Walking into the dentist on Monday, Roy walks up to the reception desk.

"Hi, my name is Roy and I have a four o'clock appointment today," says Roy.

"Yes, they are just preparing your room and will be out shortly, take a seat in the waiting lobby in the meantime," says Jane.

"This waiting makes me ponder whether or not I brushed well enough this morning," says Roy.

"I get that a lot, but brushing well the day before saves very few people," says Jane.

"Aahh, procrastination bites," says Roy going to sit down.

"Roy," says a dental hygienist standing by the entrance to the dental rooms.

Roy raises his hand and walks over to the hygienist.

"Hello Roy, my name is Cindy. Being your dental hygienist today I will clean your teeth after Dr. Thompson fixes your chipped tooth. Now, come right with me. How are you today?" says Cindy.

"Great, you see this big smile on my face, it's due to much anticipation in finding out about my poor dental habits. This is going to be a rude awakening," says Roy pointing at his wide fake smile.

***

Ten days later, Roy receives his dental bill in the mail from the dental office.

"Great teeth and whiter smile," says James while eating his supper at the kitchen table.

"You're right, they fixed my chipped tooth and cleaned my teeth bro," says Roy.

"Did you make it worth your time? The appointment didn't interfere with your jobs did it?" says James.

"I can't wait to see how much of their time it was worth? I hope my dental coverage covers most of the bill," says Roy.

"I'm sure they will cover something," says James.

"What? Look here James, it is showing a cost of four hundred and five dollars total for fixing my tooth and getting a cleaning," says Roy.

"That means you must have gotten great service with what you paid for," says James eating his bowl of rice and beans at the kitchen table.

Roy, leaning his back against the fridge says, "Life isn't fair, is it?"

"Life is very hard to control, in fact, all we have control over is our thoughts and actions. Having a good attitude and how we respond to what happens determines the outcome in the end," says James.

"Thanks for the words of wisdom, but I'm going to have to charge my credit card to pay for my bills in the months ahead. I will still pay for rent but will have to pay with credit for some of my other expenses," says Roy.

"Ah brother, this is just a temporary set back with things. Are you able to look past it and learn from it? I would advise you to pay the higher interest credit card debt off first with at least paying more than the minimum monthly payment," says James

"Learn from it, I have done everything I possibly could to keep my finances up and yet I have dug myself a hole," says Roy.

Walking over to the table, Roy sits down in a chair directly across from James.

"How do I learn about something I could do nothing about?" says Roy.

"What you have learned from this experience might be that you tried all you can, therefore, you have no regrets, you know what you can and cannot do, and you know how to manage your time effectively," says James,

"Hey, nice pep talk Vince Lombardi." says Roy.

"Now with what I have just mentioned, look at how great this experience has been for you. Try to look at how you are benefiting from the experience rather than losing in the experience itself," says James before stuffing his mouth with a big spoon full.

CHAPTER 8

"Where's Tom? James, all of the stuff in his room is gone," says Roy.

"What? What do you mean his stuff is gone?" says James.

"Look for yourself, not a single object is in his room but dust bunnies," says Roy.

"That can't be, I haven't heard or seen of him for a couple of days. I will give Tommer a call," says James dialing his cell phone.

"You know what? He ditched us and now we are left to pay the rent," says Roy.

"Just getting his voicemail, I will leave a message. Yeah Tom, I haven't talked to you in a couple of days and just checking to see if everything is alright. Why is all of your stuff gone from the apartment? Please get back to me at earliest convenience, thanks," says James.

"Oh this doesn't sit pretty well now that Tom is gone. Half the rent between the two of us is six hundred a month," says Roy.

***

Six weeks later, the brothers manage to get through their first rent payment with frugal living and working harder then ever. James has acquired a second job and their apartment looks like a mess with dirty dishes over heaping in the sink, muddy floor, and clothes thrown onto the furniture and appliances.

"It's funny Roy, over a month ago you were going crazy about your finances and now after a month's period of time, it doesn't bother you. In fact, it doesn't faze you. At first, there was a period of emotion and now it has moved into a period of adaptation or mission to become accustomed to your situation," says James.

"I see that also, but I would say it still bothers me. I just can't get over the fact that the setbacks keep happening one after the other," says Roy.

"What do you expect to come next as a setback Roy," says James.

"Well I don't have much extra money, I've become so frugal that I don't even want to buy food to eat," says Roy.

"Ah, no need to get that extensive, I'll keep the cupboards stocked," says James with a look of assurance and nodding his head.

"I need to find some extra money by cutting something that I don't need. I'm thinking about turning my cell phone plan off, which will save me an extra forty dollars per month," says Roy.

"Well, you have the right mind set to do what you need to do. Strip everything to the bones so you have the essentials and gut out what is not needed. I think you will have fun and learn by doing it," says James.

"Well, I'm glad to hear I'm on the same page," says Roy.

"Great, now lets do something to help ourselves and tackle cleaning this apartment, how does that sound?" says James.

"Let's do it," says Roy.

***

The next Monday, Roy walks into his cell phone carrier's office after working at Canet. The office is located at a section of a strip mall with glass windows making up the entire front side of the building. The front desk is towards the back of the office with a "Unicell" logo on the front of the desk. The sales floor features a big screen TV and a showcase of the latest cell phone plans available.

"I m looking to cancel my cell phone plan," says Roy.

"Okay, my name is Sharon, what is your name and address?" says Sharon standing at the customer service desk wearing a yellow "Unicell" shirt.

"I'm Roy Monte and address is 4936 28th avenue south apartment 210," says Roy.

"Shows here, your account is in good standing. What is the reason for canceling today? Do you know about our competitor price match?" says Sharon.

"I don't have the money to pay for the cell phone and need to cancel," says Roy.

"What phone will you use?" says Sharon.

"The pay phone and the phone at work," says Roy.

Sharon grins at her computer screen upon hearing this and says, "Okay, next month will be your last month. We just need you to fill out our phone termination form."

"Okay, is that all?" says Roy handing the completed form to Sharon.

"That is all, have a great day," says Sharon.

"You too," says Roy leaving the Unicell office.

***

"How did your day off go yesterday?" says Stacy at Harry's Foods.

"Much to my surprise, very efficient, in fact, now I have a whole new perspective on life and got some errands done," says Roy microwaving a frozen burrito for lunch.

"What is the new perspective about?" says Stacy.

"That no matter what happens a person can adjust to any situation." says Roy.

"Are you talking about culture shock or something?" says Stacy.

"Not really, more along the lines of a change of circumstances with the same responsibilities," says Roy now seated at the break room table allowing his burrito to cool down.

"Ah, try looking outside the box to change how you view the world," says Stacy.

"Yeah, maybe I will give that a try, what do you suggest?" says Roy.

"Perhaps, instead of viewing your circumstances altering your situation think of this as a different way to play the hand that is dealt to you," says Stacy.

"I guess I was never really good at playing card games but it does sound like a great way to make the best of any situation. Oh, by the way my phone number is no longer valid, you will no longer be able to reach me at that number," says Roy getting ready to eat his burrito.

***

The next day, Roy goes on his two day work schedule without much sleep and can finally hit his head against a pillow Saturday morning after his Canet shift. Upon waking up in the afternoon, Roy feels weak.

"Mercy, Mercy," says Roy to himself while using his arms to lift his upper body off the bed in a first of many attempts to get out of bed.

"I've never felt so weak in my entire life," says Roy walking into the kitchen.

"Hey bro what is up? How goes the fight?" says James.

"The fight is kicking my butt," says Roy with a smirk on his face.

Taking out the makings for a bowl of oatmeal, Roy microwaves up a bowl of quick oats and pours milk over the top.

"So you're going to be as frugal as possible in this stage of circumstances you are in. Living off of oatmeal, milk, rice, and beans, are going vegan?" says James.

"No, I'm not vegan, just a flexitarian. I will still eat meat occasionally. Yes, I'm quite frugal right now, if I can live without it, I will," says Roy.

"You're a pack rat Roy, living well below your means," says James.

"Yes, I will be graduating with a PhD in frugality from the University of Life Lessons.," says Roy taking a bite of his hot cereal.

CHAPTER 9

"Roy, will you come up to my office please," says Charles, Roy's supervisor on the main floor.

"Yeah sure," says Roy while checking over the conveyor belt for defective bulbs.

Roy follows Charles up the two flights of warehouse stairs to the office. Following Charles is like walking in the shadow of a giant with his big frame and long curly black hair. Most of his beard covers all the face cheeks and his largest part of the body being the mid-section protruding belly. Once inside, Roy sits in one of the two chairs in front of Charles desk.

"Roy how has your day been going so far?" says Charles.

"Great, the production line has been moving along pretty well," says Roy.

"We have a great opportunity opening up here. Sarah, the research director will be relocating to a different position. We would like to offer you the position; you've spent over a year with us and have had a great work ethic. The company feels you would have great potential looking into our future research. What do you think?" says Charles.

"When can I get started?" says Roy.

"Next week, starting Monday," says Charles.

"I accept the offer, is there a quota or job performance goal that I should consider with this position? If I could, can I receive a job description of responsibilities to be performed?"

"Yes, I will print you a job description. The pay is based on salary and with opportunities for bonuses based on the advances in our lights that take place," says Charles.

"Well, I appreciate your time Charles and what you do for the company. Now, its back to work," says Roy.

Getting out of his chair, Roy pivots on one foot and heads out of the office.

"Yes!" Roy whispers to himself enthusiastically while clenching his fist in the air.

Roy tells James the next day about his new job at Canet.

"Hey bro, guess what?" says Roy."

"Let me guess, you have come up with a way to travel back in time using the flux capacitor in the *Back to the Future* movies," says James.

"I have accepted a job promotion at Canet," says Roy.

"Well congratulations on this excellent achievement. We should celebrate by looking back at the moments these past six months have brought you," says James.

"What? Lots of sleepless nights and a lot of caffeine," says Roy.

"The amazing thing is, much of my life I have always settled for something that I did not intend to happen. I went for my degree, graduated, and could not find a job with my degree. I obtained a job in a different field and now I'm doing fair. I simply played my hand with the best I possibly could play it," says James.

"I see myself following in your foot steps," says Roy.

"What is the first item on your list with your new job?" says James.

"Pay off my credit cards and student loans," says Roy.

"How about a new car?" says James.

"Do you mean a used car?" says Roy.

"A different car, other than the piece of metal you have been driving. As far as student loans, just pay the minimum and invest the remaining extra income for long term growth," says James.

"Yeah, perhaps that would be a great idea. I will go to the car dealer after a few months of pay. I suppose I would be missing out on some capital gains in the stock market if I was giving all my money to the student loan lender," says Roy.

Roy looks at his bare hands with palms facing up and says, "I may not have been the pick of the litter, but I'm playing well with the hand that has been dealt to me."

Chapter 10

"I see," says Amanda looking into Roy's dark circled eyes sending a sudden shiver down her spine.

"What do you see when you look into my eyes?" says Roy.

Swirling a spoon around in her cup of coffee, Amanda looks down at the coffee and then looks up into his eyes. This eye contact switches three times between the cup of coffee and Roy's eyes, making her bangs shake on her forehead. She switches the swirling of the coffee in the other direction, counter clockwise.

"I see Roy serving others, trying to keep his head above water, and using his ego in order to just be like everyone else in this fast paced world," says Amanda.

"Interesting," says Roy with a smile of no surprise.

"What do you see Roy? What do you see when you look into the mirror at yourself?" says Amanda.

"Huh, never thought of it before, but now that you ask. I see a person going through a constant fight for self recognition. This person is living today for a better tomorrow getting all that he can get and using it to the best of their ability," says Roy.

"I see that also, I can relate to your point of view," says Amanda.

"You cannot relate to some of the things I have been through, have you ever been close to not having an income?" says Roy.

Amanda's eyes open with surprise, looking as if gazing through Roy at something behind him.

"You're right Roy, I had a better situation than you did upon graduating and never had to worry about money. Someone in my family from previous generations did though. That person made sure that their family would never have to endure that again. Ask yourself if that is how you want to be remembered from your immediate family?" says Amanda.

As if a light bulb lit up in Roy's mind, he meets his hands together at the fingertips with elbows on the table. He taps his finger tips together as if clapping.

"I call this the five finger applause. You see, I know you can relate with me in some ways and not so much in other ways. Any person hearing my story up to this point can tell I live a frugal life style. Just from your response, I can tell how you can relate with me. What is your story?" says Roy.

"Before we go there, I want to say that you are doing something great with your life no matter what happens to you and your working endeavor," says Amanda.

"What happened after the day we graduated from college?" says, Roy.

"I suppose you think I just retired after the graduation," says Amanda.

"You know you did better than me in school, that job you obtained was rightfully yours," says Roy.

"My favorite part was applying the skills I gained and using it to improve the profitability of my father's business," says Amanda while gazing out the window looking out to the parking lot.

CHAPTER 11

"Hi Amanda, welcome to your first day here. My name is Riley, I don't believe we've met. I'm an accountant here at Landstrom so we should be working together when the monthly budget review occurs. I bet you can't wait to manage Landstrom Tires," says Riley.

Riley is around five foot six with long blonde hair reaching his shoulders and pulled back into a pony tail. Amanda is wearing a dress shirt and kaki pants with gold earrings, which match her blond hair

"Yes Riley, I have great intentions to completely flip this company into a success," says Amanda standing up to show her short height and making a nonverbal emphasis on her intentions.

"Even to the point of getting a rank in the top ten fastest growing businesses in America?" says Riley.

"Yeah, the top ten fastest growing businesses," says Amanda.

"How do you intend to do that?" says Riley.

"Create more ways to make tires, advertise, and sell," says Amanda.

"An innovator in the making, by the way, your father would like to see you in his office immediately," says Riley.

"The man needs my advice already?" says Amanda.

"What's new?" says Riley.

Amanda walks into her glass door office with two big windows looking into the office next to the door. She sits at her desk and rests her leather brief case on the desk in front of her. A Mac desktop computer sits at her left with a desk lamp next to the monitor. Everything seems quiet at the moment. The working shift starts in a half hour with a few people sitting in their cubicles reading the newspaper headlines before their day begins. The cordless phone starts to ring sitting on the desk.

"Hello, Amanda here," says Amanda.

"Would you be so kind as to meet me in my office within the next half hour?" says Barney, Amanda's father.

"Sure Barney, I will be on the way as soon as I get my schedule done," says Amanda.

"Okay, see you then," says Barney.

"Bye," says Amanda, hanging up the phone with a curious look on her face.

"There are three versions of my dad. One, a serious person sweating the small stuff; two, a metaphorical person relating everything in life to metaphors; and three, a person of optimism. All three versions are contributors to starting this company," says Amanda to herself.

Walking into Barney's office, Amanda walks past some employee's just getting done at a meeting with Barney.

"Ah, there she is. Tell me, what time did you punch in at Amanda?" says Barney.

"You know I get a salary Barney, I don't need to punch in." says Amanda sitting down in the middle chair of the three chairs in front of Barney's desk.

"Two things I would like to discuss now. One, how will we create different ways to make new tires?" says Barney.

"Well, I have been working with some engineers from TRC Engineering and there have been some thoughts on laser cutting tires to specific sizes using a mold of liquid hot rubber being cooled. The other way is recycling tires with the powder-mix method," says Amanda.

"Tell me more about the powder-mix method," says Barney with high curious eyebrows on his face.

"Well this is a method of grinding recycled tires into powder then a hot liquid of glue and aluminum is mixed in to let cool in the tire mold," says Amanda.

"I would like to know the estimated costs of each method per set of tires, please have this on my desk by the end of the week." says Barney.

"The mold and powder mix methods are actually the cheapest per unit, they save on resources and manufacturing time. I will get you some numbers when I get back to the engineers tomorrow," says Amanda.

"Sounds like a plan; secondly, how will we create the wanting power so consumers will purchase these tires?" says Barney.

"These tires are cheaper to produce, so we can sell them for less. The glue and aluminum bonds to the rubber will make them last longer," says Amanda.

"Any other methods to get these products out onto the market?" says Barney.

"Yeah, creating a company catalog of our tires and distributing them to businesses and individuals, creating a buy three get one free sale, and offering a 60,000 mile warranty for our most durable powder mix tire," says Amanda.

"Who wouldn't like a warranty like that? I like where you are going with this Amanda. I want you to manage these new tires to the fine print. Work with the engineers and get the production line assembled in our new warehouse. Let the games begin," says Barney.

"Thanks dad," says Amanda getting out of the chair and walking through the big oak office door.

"Hi, Amanda," says a female brunette wearing kaki pants and a buttoned up shirt.

"How are you, Tori?" says Amanda.

"Great, now that I'm done with college," says Amanda.

"I bet you are glad to have some extra time to do other things. As I have heard, lifestyles after college should not change from what they were like during college," says Tori.

"I have heard that before. Do you believe it works or is it a myth?" says Amanda.

"It has to work; anything getting a person through college can get anyone through anything. However, we have all witnessed people taking up less than average careers due to the packed job market," says Tori.

"Or no job market, I once heard about a person graduating college as a police officer and working for themselves as an animal cruelty cop. The business model was set up as a non profit organization obtaining operating funds from the government and animal protection groups. The person went through thirteen years of barely making any money for themselves. All of a sudden, the relationships that this person accrued eventually created a full time job with constant business," says Amanda.

"Wow, I guess perseverance can either work for you or against you," says Tori.

"What do you mean by that?" says Amanda.

"The person persevered to the point of not getting anywhere until they ended up being in the right place at the right time. The person was not likely to all of a sudden make it big in the market and slowly built the demand from relationships," says Tori.

"Tori, what is it that you do here?" says Amanda.

"Specialty advertising and customer service/telecommunications," says Tori.

"Great, stop in my office on second floor some time today so we can cover some options for selling some new tire products," says Amanda.

"I should be able to stop in after my break this afternoon," says Tori with a big smile showing her perfect white teeth.

The two people depart and split directions in order to go back to their tasks. Tori goes to the copier and Amanda heads back to her office where the phone is ringing.

"Hey Amanda, this is Jeff calling from TRC Engineering. Those more accurate estimates for the costs of getting the machines up and running at the new warehouse will be in by next week," says Jeff.

"Sounds great as I can see how it will take a while to calculate all the specifics to something so complex," says Amanda.

"With the engineer wizards we have here, it won't be a problem. When we put two engineering heads together, we get something out of the ordinary. In relation to when they say it isn't over until the fat lady sings, well this project isn't over until everyone at TRC Engineering has put forth their idea for the product line," says Jeff.

"That is what makes TRC Engineering unique. What a way to make a good impression having some of the smartest people work together with similar capabilities," says Amanda.

"We are deciding which type of tread options to put into this mold skeleton for the machine. Which types would you like to include?" says Jeff.

"I would like to include the all season, icy road, burnout, and decal design with company logo in the tread," says Amanda.

"Interesting, you put the company logo in the tread of the tire," says Jeff.

"Yes, actually the logo design is quite good for traction on the road," says Amanda.

"We would like to get to the new warehouse and obtain some measurements for the machine. By the way, the designers of this machine will call it "Burnout". I have to get going now, I have some more products to design," says Jeff.

"Have a good day," says Amanda hanging up the phone.

By late afternoon, Tori walks into her office with a brief case. She sits in one of the two chairs in front of the desk.

"Okay, I have brainstormed a list of options for the new tires. There's the frequent customer free tire promotion, satisfaction guaranteed or your money back, and buy one get one fifty percent off phone call," says Tori.

"What is the typical number of purchases for phone call and electronic advertisements?" says Amanda.

"The best outlook we can look at achieving is about ten to fifteen percent. That's if we place our cards right using a target market of previous customers," says Tori.

"What will it take in funding to get this advertising up and running?" says Amanda.

"It's important to consider a product's life cycle when considering the funding used. The early stages in the product's life will not be as demanding, so advertising will create the demand for it. When the product life cycle peaks, demand will be high and more products will be bought. Think of a product's life cycle like a rocket. A lot of fuel is required to get a rocket off the ground and into the air. Once it gets going in the air, not as much fuel is required when compared to take off. Most of our funding will go to advertising and getting a position in the market," says Tori.

"I see, once we create the demand for the product, then most of our focus is getting the product out the door at the peak of the product cycle," says Amanda.

"Yes," says Tori with an affirming nod.

The phone rings and Amanda reaches her hand over the phone.

"That cover's it today Tori have a great day," says Amanda.

"Yep," says Tori initiating momentum to get up out of the chair and walking out of the glass office door.

Chapter 12

Standing in the dead office space on the second floor, Barney and Amanda are next to the vending machine at the stairwell exit door. Trying to pick which Gatorade to get, Barney taps his index finger on his chin.

"How has Sam been lately? I haven't seen him since the graduation," says Barney pushing the red Gatorade button.

"He's still busy with his real estate business. Seems like he is always on his toes and always doing something to improve. He starts work at 5:30 in the morning and later gets done at 5:30 in the evening only to do a few hours of work writing his next novel," says Amanda.

"Reminds me of myself at his age living to work," says Barney.

"Yeah, it takes its toll on our relationship. I think he is a great guy but he must know the concept of living a balanced life, says Amanda.

Barney and Amanda walk across the big cubicle room to where Barney's office is.

"I have great news Amanda, the advertising being done by Tori has initiated a demand twice that of our other products and sales are good," says Barney.

"Wow, do sales look to stay consistent? We have been doing advertising for the past six months," says Amanda.

"Much of the sales, about sixty percent have been from business accounts and they look to add these new tires to their product line. Amanda, this is great for business. You've been working hard to get some new tire products in the company. These new tires not only increased our revenue, they also reduced our expenses and improved time efficiency," says Barney.

"That is what I like to hear. I've always wanted to help make the world a better place," says Amanda.

"You are, I have added ten new jobs to the company and made several more business investments with a couple of round lots in the stock market. I've decided to give you a bonus for the great performance in the recent months," says Barney.

"Wow, a bonus is always good. What do you think about when it comes to investing in the stock market for the company?" says Amanda.

"There should be a spot for short term money and long tern money in your accounts whether it be for business or individual use. Any money put into the stock market should stay there for at least fifteen years so you can get a decent return back after government taxes," says Barney.

"What percent of your funds will be for long term and short term?" says Amanda.

"Instead of going by percent, I go by having enough to pay company bills. There should be enough cash reserves in short term bank accounts for six to twelve months of expenses, so the rest can be put into long term investments," says Barney.

"Of course, even the short term cash account is not touched most of the time," says Amanda.

"Ideally, yes." says Barney.

"I really appreciate the bonus dad, this will only make me work harder to improve results and make the profit building a routine occurrence," says Amanda.

Amanda keeps a pen to note book paper, writing some notes of topics being covered in the meeting. She gets her cup of coffee close to her mouth but doesn't take a sip with an idea suddenly coming to her mind.

"How do you deal with risk in a business like this father?" says Amanda.

"When I started this business twenty-five years ago, I put eighty percent of my life savings into it. Now, if that isn't risky, nothing is. The thing with risk is that the more risk a person assumes, the more benefits or losses likely to occur. I had some money built up and if I had lost all the money invested in this business, I probably would have been done putting my money at risk for a while," says Barney.

"The company doesn't put eighty percent of profit money at high risk, do they?" says Amanda.

"Good question, we do not put it at high risk. You see, I like the power of three, a third of our money is put to higher risk growth stocks, a third for stock with a good reputation or blue chips, and a third is put into bonds," says Barney.

This time, Amanda gets the chance to drink some of her coffee before coming up with a new topic of conversation.

"What would you say about borrowing money for the new tire designs we are implementing?" says Amanda.

"Borrowing money has differences, I mean there is a difference between good debt and bad debt, short term and long term debt. In my business I look at long term debt being good because the interest rate can be lower, and the item is less likely to be a purchase based on impulse," says Barney.

Taking his glasses off and resting them in there folded position on the table; Barney gives Amanda a right eye wink.

"Do you remember when I used to give you a right eye wink when you were little? Every time you came home from day care, running up the stairs to my home office I would give you a right eye wink and ask you, 'what was the highlight of your day?'" says Barney.

"Yes, I remember that, you would always tell me to knock first before coming into the office, but I would storm in anyway," says Amanda.

"Back to the topic, there is a difference between using good credit and bad credit when borrowing money. Good credit would be a business loan from a bank; bad credit would be using the credit card for business purchases. Borrowing money also has risk in comparison between how much money a business has and how much they borrow. We borrow no more than twenty-five percent of our cash reserves to maintain a healthy amount of debt that isn't too much," says Barney.

"Do you have a credit card to use with the company?" says Amanda.

"No, I have seen businesses do well by using credit cards to finance their purchases though. As long as they pay the balance off right away, a business that does a lot of traveling will save money to pay for airlines in this way," says Barney.

"What do you suppose to be Landstrom Tires biggest

weakness? What are you doing to prevent regression and down sizing in the future?" says Amanda.

"Oh, I'm sure being questioned today, aren't I? Landstrom's biggest weakness is success, not failure, success. Some things are just too good to be true, deciding between a risk that is too good to be true and one that is reasonable can make or break a business," says Barney.

"Having more stuff is not always better. Business can either be down with little growth or business can be good to the point of getting too big to keep track of everything occurring. Pick your poison," says Amanda.

"Growth organized well can lead to success with the right team and delegation present. Well, I have some work to do. In the mean time, let me know of any ideas that you have in extending the new tire line sales peak and sales after the peak occurs," says Barney.

"I will come up with a strategy by next Tuesday, wait until you see my plan," says Amanda with a look of reassurance.

Barney nods with understanding and Amanda stands with her notebook and pen in each hand. Walking past the solid oak office door, Amanda grabs the door handle with her pen in hand and closes the door as she walks out.

CHAPTER 13

"Sam are you home?" says Amanda as she walks into the apartment.

The apartment's white painted walls with grape vine wallpaper give an Italian style look. The kitchen and island countertop is located right next to the front door with the living room to the far side of the front door next to the bathroom and two bedrooms.

"Hello Amanda," says Sam walking in the front door.

"You must have got home just moments after me," says Amanda, looking into Sam's blue eyes.

Sam's brown hair and blue eyes show a side of intimidation and seriousness with no expression.

"What's wrong Sam?" says Amanda.

"Nothing, I just have great news. I got promoted today!" says Sam with both fists high in the air, looking up at the ceiling.

"Great, let's celebrate, I have some wine that I have been saving for a while," says Amanda walking into the living room to get a look at the T.V. guide in the newspaper.

"Sounds great, will you check my laptop computer to see if I have any e-mails in my inbox? My laptop is sitting on the coffee table," says Sam.

"Yeah, sure thing," says Amanda sitting on the couch in front of the coffee table.

Opening up the laptop computer, Sam positions himself standing behind the couch looking at the computer screen with Amanda.

"Sam what's this? Oh my," says Amanda.

Holding open hands to her mouth, Amanda reads from an already open document.

"Amanda, will you marry me?"

A picture of the engagement ring is just below the written proposal in the computer document.

Sam walks up to Amanda and with that serious look with no expression again, kneels to one knee and shows Amanda the actual engagement ring from the picture.

"Amanda Landstrom, will you marry me?" says Sam.

"Yes, Yes I will marry you," says Amanda dropping to both knees from sitting on the couch and hugging Sam.

The big hug makes Amanda's head a few inches below Sam's so that her eyes are at Sam's chin level. Amanda's forehead is touching the side of Sam's cheek then a parting of Amanda's head from Sam's occurs. Amanda looks up into Sam's eyes.

"Sam, does my father know you intended to propose to me just now?" says Amanda.

"No, I was thinking we could do that the next time we stop in to visit your folks," says Sam with a weak voice as if not looking forward to doing it.

"My father is very traditional, and will need to be given lots of reasons why we should be together," says Amanda.

"I get along great with him, but ever since I accidentally broke his grandfather's clock, he views me as bad luck.

Almost to the point of me deserving to be tarred and feathered," says Sam.

"He can get over it. I think he likes you more than you think," says Amanda.

A couple weeks later, Amanda and Sam stop into Father Barney Landstrom's home, a three floor brick home and a three stall garage. Every light is on in the house, three new vehicles in the garage stalls, and Barney is in the front yard looking at stars through his telescope.

"Hey, I was just thinking about you two. What brings you here?" says Landstrom.

"Dad, Sam and I have been together since the first year of college, and I want to say that we are getting married," says Amanda.

Sam looks at Amanda as if she created a scene of personal information falling into the wrong hands.

"I guess what ever makes each of you happy, you will make each other complete in life's pursuit of service, ingenuity, and happiness," says Barney with hands clasped behind his back to communicate openness.

"A quality marriage correlates much with service, ingenuity, and happiness," says Amanda.

"I'm okay with you getting married Amanda, and I do want to see you achieve everything you can and take all you can get," says Barney.

"You know me dad, I'm always on the look out for the next opportunity and the next hidden gem," says Amanda.

"Speaking of gems, can I see the rock?" says Barney.

"Certainly," says Amanda, holding up the ring for her father to see as the three stand in the darkness of the front yard.

"Amazing, isn't it? Something so small can symbolize something as big as life long marriage," says Barney looking closely at the ring near his face.

"I practically dug to the center of the earth to obtain that piece of rock. It is totally worth it though, I wouldn't question the effort for what it is worth to me," says Sam

"Well, I predict the reason why you came here today is to inform me of your engagement. I truly am happy for the both of you. Amanda, I suggest you tell your mother about the engagement in the house. Now, let me get back to finding a rare star that only shows up every century," says Barney looking through his telescope.

While inside the house, Amanda tells her mother Julia about the engagement with intense excitement while stiffening her body to show enthusiasm. Sam makes the decision to stand outside quietly with Barney looking for his star.

"Ah ha, there she be, I found it. Boy is it small," says Barney.

"I know I should have asked permission to marry your daughter first before proposing," says Sam.

"Even if I would've disagreed, might it have altered you asking her?" says Barney.

"Well, no I guess," says Sam.

"How well do you know of Amanda's personal life?" says Barney.

"Of course, I have been living with her for more than a year," says Sam.

"At the age of eight Amanda's great grandfather past away with his will stating one third of his retirement monies be put in his grandchildren's name equally. The only grand child of his was Amanda and he had one point three million dollars in his retirement account. Amanda had the money transferred into an IRA of her own, giving her a total of over four hundred thousand dollars at the time," says Barney.

"Wow, I would never have thought that was the case," says Sam.

"Sam, she will not touch that money until she retires, only way she will touch that money is if it's her last resort," says Barney clenching his hand into a fist and shaking it next to his ear.

"I understand totally," says Sam.

"So don't get any crazy ideas about what to do with it," says Barney.

"Hey, it's not my money and there's nothing I can do to deserve that amount of money," says Sam.

"Yes there is Sam, take care and love my daughter until the day you die. Please look after her when I'm gone," says Barney.

"It will be a while before that happens," says Sam.

"My blood pressure is higher than ever and my medication doesn't seem to help any. I should have watched my diet a little better during all these years, but long term habits are the number one killer today," says Barney.

Let's go inside," says Sam resting his hand on Barney's shoulder as they both turn around and enter into the big house through the solid oak front door.

Chapter 14

A week after getting married, Sam and Amanda are ready for their first home.

"Well, I like the interior of this home and it is located just a block away from my office, what a great location," says Amanda.

"Yeah, the backyard patio would be a great place for my Kingsford Grill. This home is only four years old, with plenty of space to move around," says Sam looking around the house with a vision of great interest of what could be.

"We'll take it," says Sam and Amanda in unison after looking each other in the eyes

The realtor looks surprised from such a quick big decision and not even looking to negotiate a lower price.

"I think we have a new record," says the surprised realtor.

***

With Barney in a contractor proposal meeting the next morning covering all terrain testing for a new line of tires, Amanda and John wait outside the meeting room. John, a long time friend of Barney's, mentions some ideas to Amanda.

"With this new line of tires we are introducing to the market, what is the expected income to come from these tires?" says John who's bald head reflects off the lights above.

"The expectation is to increase income by one third, I believe it has the potential to increase by up to fifty percent," says Amanda.

"What will happen to this additional chunk of change at the company?" says John.

"We will invest most of it into stocks and bonds for higher rates of return," says Amanda.

Having a smile on his face, John uses his thumb and index finger to pinch his nose for a second. Flexing his knee, he taps his left foot on the floor behind him.

"Did you hear that? What was your impression of what I just did?" says John.

"Yes, you tapped your foot on the floor behind you," says Amanda.

"Anything that occurs behind us is something we cannot see. If we can't see it, we can't fully understand it. What is occurring behind this company? What is occurring behind its back?" says John.

"I guess I'm not fully aware of that, but I'm doing everything I can to help get the company where it needs to be," says Amanda.

"What are you doing right now Amanda?" says John.

"I'm being all that I can be, John. You see, I see myself as a one person army. Fighting fire with fire and cutting diamonds with diamonds," says Amanda.

"Ha, cutting diamonds with diamonds, never heard of that one before," says John surprisingly.

John transitions from a closed posture of arms crossing at the chest and foot stance close together to an open posture of arms behind back and foot stance wider than shoulder width apart.

"So, are you claiming to be a cure all? To be the person who takes away all my worries and solves all the company's problems?" says John.

"I cannot do that, as much as I would like to, I can't," says Amanda.

'Amanda, we are a team here and the next time you have another "one person army episode" remember that,' says John.

"One person army? Do we have an Alexander the Great among us?" says Barney among the first to leave the meeting room.

"A cure all Alexander the Great to be exact," says John to Barney.

"No person can be too great, but they can be too big. The number one killer to a business is success leading to an unnecessary growth," says Barney.

"Well that is all she wrote today, have a good day," says Amanda leaving John and Barney in the office finishing up the conversation.

***

Amanda's ride home to pick up Sam is filled with anticipation as they are going to shop for a new car today.

"Ready to go have a shopping fiesta honey?" says Amanda parking the car in the talking to Sam shoveling snow in the drive way.

"Let the price negotiating begin," says Sam.

"What's our price limit for this one?" says Amanda.

"Twenty-five grand would be below our means on this one." says Sam climbing into the new 1999 Chevy Trailblazer.

At Merk's Mercury dealership, Merk shows the new 2000 Mercury car model.

"Nice car, take care of it and it will take care of you the next fifteen years. If you want a long lasting, low maintenance vehicle here it is," says Merk.

"Looks great, what is the price for a car like this?" says Sam.

"Twenty four thousand five hundred," says Merk.

"With the recent Mercury recall to the common faulty suspension, I will give you twenty-one grand for it," says Sam.

"Just consider the twenty four grand on the price sticker with this money. Let's say you take three hundred trips with this car every year for ten years, and then you decide to get a new car. Over ten years, this costs eight dollars a trip, which is pretty good. Do you think that is pretty good?" says Merk.

"Yes, that does seem pretty good, but my option would be the lowest common denominator. What does twenty one grand total to be per trip?" says Sam.

"Twenty one grand would give us about seven dollars a trip over ten years. Look here, I believe a person gets what they pay for and this car is worth twenty four grand. Let's do a win-win situation. My final offer is twenty three grand," says Merk.

Amanda and Sam look at each other and come to a nonverbal agreement by knowing what each other is thinking and nodding a gesture to conclude the nonverbal communication.

"I would like to think about it first, twenty two thousand five hundred dollars seems like a more even win-win situation to me. I guess we will come back later today if we have made a decision on the car. Have a great day and thanks for showing us around," says Amanda.

"You're welcome any time," says Merk with arms out wide with palms up and Amanda and Sam departing for their Trailblazer outside.

At Jeff's Your Way or The Highway used car dealer, there is a similar selection of vehicles with over one hundred vehicles to choose from. The location is on a hill with a top selection of cars and bottom section of trucks and SUV's. Bottom and top sections have a flat area built into the hill with the main office on the top tier and a road going down to the bottom tier from the top.

"Well, what do you think of this one Amanda?" says Sam looking over and pointing at a new Chevy Impala.

"That black one with the moon roof? How about the Chevy Malibu next to it?" says Amanda.

"I like the black one, let's get out and look," says Sam, unlocking the door and putting the vehicle in park.

"Wow, it's only has ten thousand miles on it and is a year old," says Amanda noticing a sales person walking up to talk.

"Hello, how are you on this fine day? My name is Winston. I bet your day will be even better after taking that Impala for a test drive," says Winston.

"Let's take it for a drive, hop in Sam," says Amanda opening the driver door.

"With the improved crash test rating and all wheel braking system this car is sure to be the best choice for your family," says Winston.

Driving off in the car, Amanda makes her way down the hill to the main road turning into the dealership. The end of the hill is where the intersection meets the dealership entrance and that is where Amanda decides to test the breaks. The car comes to a quick and easy stop that is silently smooth.

"Wow, it's like there is a bungee cord attached from behind to slow us down. So this is a 2001 model black Impala? Nice!" says Amanda.

"Yeah, I think we can get Winston to come down a few thousand to nineteen grand, they usually have about fifteen percent to play with for markup," says Sam.

"Let's experience everything life has to offer and get this car. We can afford it with all of my recent bonuses," says Amanda.

"Ah, there is much out there that life has to offer, we shall have the best of the best," says Sam.

Coming back to the dealership, Amanda and Sam pull the car up to the office after revving hard on the gas peddle up the hill. Winston is waiting outside of the dealership office talking on his phone.

"I know this is the right truck for you and your farm needs. There is more than enough power to get up and down the Black Hills of South Dakota with your camper, stop down today and we can go over more in detail," says Winston talking on the phone.

"Look we can only afford a financing option of nineteen grand due to the second line of equity on our house. The twenty one thousand nine hundred ninety-nine is not a comparable option given our situation," says Sam.

"Do you like the easy maneuvering and all wheel braking?" says Winston after hanging up his cell phone.

"Yes, I like the look and the drive," says Amanda.

"This is the car to make your day wonderful, which features something that will last. That feature is value, value is not only something you want, but also experiencing everything life has to offer," says Winston.

Amanda looks across the hood of the car at Sam standing next to the passenger door. Both recall their conversation just earlier about experiencing all that life has to offer.

"That's odd," says Sam.

"What's odd?" says Winston.

"Nothing," says Sam.

"Twenty grand is my offer and we'll give you each a coupon for one oil change at our auto shop," says Winston.

"Oh, it really is your way or the highway here, sounds fair as I know how dealerships make it in today's world. Twenty grand it is," says Amanda.

"Great, now let's go fill out the paper work in my office," says Winston walking over to the front door.

Driving away in their new car, Amanda and Sam have taken the next step in living their dream.

"With this car purchase and the home we just bought, what is next on the list of toys to buy?" says Amanda.

"Well there is always the lake cabin, a good cash generator, or a motorcycle," says Sam.

"The lake cabin is nice, there is one thing I noticed with the car," says Amanda.

"What's that?" says Sam.

"There are no sub speakers in this car. I listen to good music and good music needs a good speaker if I'm going to listen to it. Let's take it to the auto detail shop on Main Avenue to get some speakers," says Amanda.

"A welcome addition to add some pizzazz to this vehicle," says Sam.

At the auto detail shop on Main Avenue, the place is busy with many customizations taking place. The classic street show coming up next week will have classic muscle cars on display.

"Hi, my name is Amanda and I would like to have some sub speakers put into my Impala," says Amanda to the women at the customer service counter.

"We have three kinds in stock right now: the T200, T1000, and T2000," says the customer service rep with Julie printed on her name tag.

"Let's go with the T1000, as I feel the T200 is going to be too small," says Amanda.

"Okay that will be five hundred nineteen dollars and twenty-two cents, when will you have the repairs done?" says Julie.

"Today or as soon as possible, when is the soonest you can get it done?" says Amanda.

"I can get it in on Monday and possibly be done by Tuesday," says Julie.

"Great, Yes I will be in on Tuesday to get the car, or just let me know when it is ready," says Amanda.

"Sounds great," says Julie with Amanda leaving the key to the car on the front desk and walking out the front door.

***

Come Tuesday, Amanda has been without a car for two days and cannot stand being given a ride to everywhere she needs to go: work, the tanning spa, the gym, and the grocery store. Calling on her cell phone to the auto detail shop, she is looking to pick up her vehicle today.

"Main avenue Auto Detail Shop, this is Julie how can I help you?" says Julie on the other line.

"Hi, this is Amanda I'm checking to see when my Impala will be finished today," says Amanda.

"The Impala is waiting to be installed right now, we will call you when we are done with the installation," says Julie.

"Yes, thanks for your help," says Amanda hanging up the cell phone.

***

"It's Thursday now and I have not heard yet from the detail shop on my car," says Amanda sitting across from Sam at their big oak kitchen table.

"I think they would've been able to get to it by now, and it would be nice to have the car tomorrow when we head out on our trip out of state," says Sam.

"I'll give them a call, they should still be open," says Amanda dialing her cell phone.

"Hi this is Amanda, there is a 2000 black Impala in your shop getting sub-speakers installed, what is its status?" says Amanda.

"We have been busy this week with the upcoming classic

street show and we should be able to look at it by the end of this week," says Julie.

"You've been looking at it for the entire week," says Amanda.

"I understand, we will look at it as soon as possible," says Julie.

"Can I get money back for the time your shop has cost me, time is money you know," says Amanda.

"I apologize for any inconveniences this may have caused Amanda. We will contact you shortly when it is done, have a great day," says Julie.

"See you in a bit," says Amanda hanging up the phone.

CHAPTER 15

"Now that we have this big house we should fill it with a bunch of possessions and goodies," says Amanda sitting at the dinner table looking around at the open room space.

"You are right dear, what would you suggest to liven up the place," says Sam this time sitting next to Amanda.

"I seen this big TV and hot tub while shopping the other day, and you know a couple of children will always add some noise and excitement," says Amanda.

"Children? Now?" says Sam with a look of surprise.

"Let's think big and go for it all. Let's live life to the fullest. Purchasing these items and having a bun in the oven is realistically achievable right now," says Amanda.

"Of course, if a person can think of it, then it's achievable," says Sam.

"Let's go right now to Sears and see what there is," says Amanda.

Amanda and Sam get into their new Impala after finishing dinner and head to Sears.

***

"Welcome to Sears, can I help you with anything today," says the customer service representative.

"Yes, we are looking for a TV and hot tub, what do you have available?" says Sam.

"Ah, I've noticed you staring at the fifty-two inch TV. We offer free delivery this month and a fifty dollar mail in rebate," says the customer service rep.

"Great, we'll take it," says Amanda.

"The best hot tub we have in stock is the Turbo Jet 3000. I'm sure you have some aches and pains that you want to alleviate," says the customer service rep to the couple as they walk there way to the bath appliance section.

Looking at the Turbo Jet 3000 leaning up against the wall, it was big enough for four people to use. Out of the three hot tubs on display, it was the biggest one available.

"Looks great, what do you think Sam?" says Amanda.

"I like the power jets for my upper back and by the looks of this one, there are plenty jets," says Sam.

"We'll take it," says Amanda.

"That comes to be $4,522.99 for the TV and hot tub. We will have them delivered to your house tomorrow," says the customer service rep standing at the checkout.

"My Credit card limit is fifteen hundred dollars, is there a financing option?" says Amanda.

"Yes, we have no interest for six months," says the customer service rep.

"Okay, let's go with putting a grand down today on the credit card," says Amanda.

With the new TV and hot tub arriving the next day, Amanda and Sam enjoy the big screen TV and hot tub hours later. With the lights dim and a silent night at the back patio deck, Amanda and Sam enjoy a relaxing night in the hot tub.

"Sam, I have a kink in my neck all of the time from being at the office," says Amanda with a frown on her face.

"The combo of a jet massage and a neck rub will do the trick," says Sam positioning himself to be seated next to Amanda in hot tub.

"What will be the happiest day in your life?" says Amanda relaxed from Sam's neck massage.

"I will be the happiest the day I can say my love for you lasted a lifetime," says Sam.

"Oh, that's so sweet, you'll never get rid of me. For better or for worse, right?" says Amanda.

"Crystal clear," says Sam.

"Another thing, I have been so busy at the office I have no time to clean this big house now. I have put on some extra weight from the stress I'm under, any ideas?" says Amanda.

"A way to solve that problem could be getting a house made to do the cleaning and getting a personal trainer to get your weight under control," says Sam.

"Do you think that's affordable?" says Amanda.

"I see house maids in classifieds all the time for twelve hundred a month and some even less. I bet there will be a personal trainer at Jerry's Gym on 7th Street. You know, we do have a gym membership there," says Sam.

"Oh yeah, I forgot all about that. It's been over three weeks since I've been there," says Amanda.

***

A week later, the newly hired house maid arrives in the afternoon for a quick look at the house. With professional business attire and suit case, Gwen the house maid looks over the house.

"Great to see you here on time and as you can see the opportunity is here for plenty of work," says Amanda standing at the kitchen counter.

"Oh, yes I will get this place spic and span in no time," says Gwen sliding her first two fingers on top of the living room mantle to accumulate a visible amount of dust on her finger.

"Here is a key to the front door, please keep the door locked. When will you be arriving to clean?" says Amanda with eyebrows high with curiosity.

"I should be able to be by around ten in the morning," says Gwen pulling out her schedule from her brief case to look at the openings she has.

"That will be great and your check will be sent to you every month by mail," says Amanda.

"I shall be going now," says Gwen.

"You have no idea how much of a life saver you will be for us," says Amanda.

"I hear that a lot," says Gwen walking out the front door.

***

Walking through a single glass door at Jerry's Gym, a big buff man is sitting at the front desk. Amanda approaches the desk with intimidation.

"Do you offer personal training here at the gym," says Amanda.

"We do, my name is Drew, a personal trainer here. One of my clients recently dropped forty pounds with my Fab

Five Interval Circuit. See for yourself," says Drew pointing to a poster of the before and after photo of one of his clients.

"Wow can you whip me into that great a shape?" says Amanda.

"A person can do anything they put their mind to. With just two sessions a week, I can get you on track to achieving that goal weight you're looking for," says Drew.

"I would like to do a three month training program two times a week. Keep me going and push me until I lose my twenty pounds of extra weight," says Amanda.

"Do you have time to get started today? Why wait until tomorrow what you can do today?" says Drew.

"Yes, I do have my workout clothes with me. I should be ready to go, just give me ten minutes," says Amanda.

"Okay, is this your first personal training session?" says Drew.

"Yes" says Amanda.

"What does the word fascinate mean to you?" says Drew.

"I guess it means something good that was not expected," says Amanda.

"To me, fascinate means bringing out the best in a person. Exercise brings out the best in everyone and I bet you can do more than you think," says Drew.

Going directly to the treadmill, Amanda starts with walking to warm up.

"Now, let's hit the trenches with some resistance exercise," says Drew walking next to Amanda to the free weight area.

"I bet you have been through this workout a thousand times," says Amanda.

"Sort of yes and no, I will be adding a couple of different exercises to the workout today. To start, we are going to do a basement lunge and then an interval of jumping rope. Do you like to jump rope?" says Drew.

"Yeah, but I bet my timing during the jump is going to be off, it has been a long time since doing this," says Amanda.

"Just do what you can do, and believe you can do it" says Drew.

Amanda surprisingly realizes she can do more than she thought. This resistance and cardio exercise combo continues until the middle of the workout.

"I will be counting backwards from ten reps to one rep as we alternate between doing pushups and sit-ups. For example, we will do ten pushups and ten sit-ups followed by nine pushups and nine sit-ups until we get to completing one pushup and one sit-up," says Drew.

"What if I can't do ten right away?" says Amanda.

"Ask your self instead, what if I can't do ten reps right away? Expect the best results and you will get the best results, so let's begin," says Drew.

"Ten push ups….Ten sit-ups, piece of cake," says Amanda.

"How are you doing?" says Drew acting as a spotter with about three reps remaining in the pyramid drop set.

"Tell me again why I signed up for this. My arms feel like Jell-O," says Amanda.

"You are doing this to fit into those same pair of clothes you wore a few years ago. You can do it, never give up, never surrender," says Drew.

"Last rep, can I choose mercy?" says Amanda.

"You've come too far to give up now," says Drew.

By the end of the workout, Amanda is slow to move compared to when she started the workout.

"Amanda, do you have a spring in your step?" says Drew as Amanda stretches on a floor mat to loosen her tight muscles.

"There's not much left if there is. Reminding me of floor mats, one time at a family gathering my rice dish spilt in the car on the way there. I had to serve half of the remaining dish not spilt and every called my rice dish, "floor mat rice" just to tease me," says Amanda.

"That's hilarious, great job today Amanda. Outside of today's session do three more days of cardio on your own. What days can you come in to complete that?" says Drew with an expression of laughter.

"Monday's, Thursday's, and Sunday's work best in the evening after I do the household chores," says Amanda.

"Monday, Thursday, and Sunday it is, now commit to it. I will see you at the next session," says Drew putting away his clipboard and nodding his head to confirm the session's completion.

Chapter 16

"Amanda, have you heard?" says Janice over the phone.

"Janice so good to hear from you, I was thinking about meeting with you about the next growth investment worth considering for my portfolio," says Amanda.

"No need to cover that today we need to consider that THT Industry stock purchased a couple of years ago," says Janice.

"What happened?" says Amanda.

"The original investment of one hundred eleven dollars per share is now worth one hundred ninety-eight dollars a share. Amanda, you purchased five hundred shares. What was once fifty-five grand is now worth ninety-nine grand," says Janice.

"Wow, I did not think the shares would grow that quickly, would you suggest selling the stock?" says Amanda.

"It's a good idea to just wait it out even if the stock decides to drop some. This is a company stock that is not very volatile, so there should not be any expected changes," says Janice.

"If the stock goes below one fifty-five per share, I want you to sell to make sure I get my investment back," says Amanda.

"I urge you to stay the course and hold this investment for the future potential that it holds," says Janice.

"Good point, I guess I was just acting on emotions and impulse again," says Amanda.

"I will sell at one hundred fifty, how does that sound? Should give this valuable stock a second chance, and who doesn't deserve a second chance?" says Janice.

"Okay, you have an agreement. What is the beta or volatility of the stock right now? Is it more or less than one?" says Amanda.

"The Beta is one point sixty six, so it's a little volatile right now even though the market has been rising," says Janice.

"How have my other stock holdings been?" says Amanda twirling the phone cord around her finger.

"Baggat is at a record high with there new line of software becoming a big hit to consumers. With your five hundred Baggat shares, they're up thirty dollars per share from where you purchased them. Massac is going into a down phase from the price we purchased a couple of years ago. With more competitors world wide, the company's earnings have gone down ten dollars per share," says Janice.

"Two out of three is not a bad deal, after all, the world is not perfect," says Amanda.

"Right, I believe you have a reputation for success. One that is going to come through during both bull and bear markets," says Janice.

"Well, I have to get going, talk to you later," says Amanda hanging up the phone.

"Well, what did Janice have to say?" says Sam sitting across the living room in a recliner.

"Most of my stock is up a good amount," says Amanda.

"Was the conversation thorough or did you forget to tell Janice something again?" says Sam.

"I guess I could have explained how I planned on making more soldiers, also known as stock investments. Eventually, I want to get to the point of making an army work for me," says Amanda.

"This isn't war Amanda, maybe you should try to view it as the farmer planting seeds and later harvesting the crop," says Sam.

"That's too boring and besides I'm a growth investor, I need to think a little aggressive. The farmer planting seeds mentality is more of an income investor," says Amanda.

"Does more risk, come with less certainty?" says Sam.

"More risk is the only way we will create the future that we want. A person getting one percent from their bank savings account will not get anywhere significant in their lifetime. The only certainty no risk creates is staying in the same place and I don't like that," says Amanda.

"Ah, that mind set is of a champion, you should be on a Wheaties box," says Barney entering the living room.

"Dad, you're up, didn't think you could sleep so late," says Amanda.

"Yeah, after what happened last night I think I'm about due," says Barney.

"I bet the bad weather coming from the airport was a long slow drive," says Sam.

"There was so much snow coming down, I could not see where I was going half the time," says Barney.

"I did not think you would make it after they issued the no travel advisory and I don't think a snow plow could have made it out to your place in the country side," says Amanda.

"When your mother picked me up at the airport, we were contemplating about staying there. I figured we could always turn around and head back if things look grim," says Barney.

"By the way, is mom still sleeping?" says Amanda.

"She's in the shower," says Barney.

"I can't wait to see the new ring you got her dad," says Amanda.

"One of my favorites is when you were just a kid Amanda. We went down to the Tulson Hill to go sledding and the first time going down the hill you wiped out and went face first into the snow. Huh, when you got up you looked like frosty the snowman," says Barney with a grin on his face.

"Okay, who is going to shovel the snow off the side walk and push snow off the driveway?" says Amanda.

"Last nose goes," says Barney putting his index finger on his nose.

"Huh, Sam it's you, you were last to touch your nose," says Amanda.

"Alright, someone has to do it," says Sam.

"The best place to start is at the front door Sam," says Barney.

"Good idea, I'll be sure not to shovel the snow into the wind," says Sam.

"To my understanding, we're in a bull market. Plentiful, everything is, I remember my grandfather losing almost everything in the stock market during the great depression. He was among few who decided to hold tight and not sell his shares. When I asked him why he didn't, he said it's because there was no influence on how he was going to live his lifestyle. You see, he had a job to pay the bills and taking his money out would just make him start over," says Barney.

"Where did that decision leave him thirty years later?" says Amanda.

"That decision made him over fifty grand richer during his retirement," says Barney.

"Okay, that does it. How about we go rock, paper, and scissors for the snow shoveling? The best two out of three," says Sam.

"You lost pal, now chop chop," says Barney.

Heading outside, Sam pulls his stocking cap over his ears and turns on the outside light next to the front door and garage. Barney and Amanda are left in the living room, which is dimly lit by two table lamps. The darkness of the living room is darker than the gray light of day break beaming through the windows.

"How has your relationship with Sam been Amanda?" says Barney with thumb and forefinger pinching his chin.

"Great, I see him playing more of a conservative role in our relationship, he always expresses that I should slow down and not be as aggressive with my actions," says Amanda.

"Perhaps, he has experienced regression with his own aggressive actions in the past and wants you to realize the same," says Barney.

"Risk, he works in real estate, so his line of business is a lot more risky than what I do. With a market downturn, the housing market can collapse, his assets and business can hit rock bottom," says Amanda.

"Do you think Sam has a plan in place if the worse case scenario does happen? I think Sam is more prepared than you think. Back in the early seventies when my business was slow progressing, I got an evening job working thirty-two hours a week. Two years I did this and finally, my revenues gained just enough for me to provide for myself," says Barney.

"That was very courageous of you to do that dad," says Amanda.

"What I'm saying is, if a person works harder than anyone else to get what they want, and they know what it is that they want in fine detail. Impossible is nothing. Oh, hi Chels," says Barney, recognizing his wife Chelsey entering the room.

"Did you find out about the road conditions, I want to get home because I forgot my loaf of banana bread on the counter," says Chelsey with white curly hair and wearing a red bath robe.

"I suppose you thought you'll be returning soon," says Amanda.

"Yes, it wasn't snowing when I left the house and once I got to the air port it was snowing fiercely," says Chelsey.

"I want to see your new ring. How big is the rock?" says Amanda transitioning her eyes to Chelsey's hand.

"We'll say there is more than a caret of diamond on this one," says Chelsey holding up her right hand with the new ring.

Amanda's eyes grow big as she examines the diamond up close. Sam enters through the front door with snow covering his legs from the knees down.

"The streets should be plowed enough for possible travel," says Sam.

"Okay, let's get going dear. It was all great that you let us be your guests for the emergency stay," says Chelsey.

"Any time," says Sam after entering through the front door with snow boots.

Barney and Chelsey ready to embark with their winter apparel and head out the door. Waiving a good bye gesture, Barney gives a peace signal with his hand before closing the door behind him.

CHAPTER 17

"Where should we go out to eat tonight dear?" says Sam while getting into the Impala with Amanda.

"Well, there is Benny's Fine and Dine and Picarso's Italian Restaurant. How about that new sea food place? I think its Sergie's Sea Food, my friend says they have good tilapia," says Amanda.

"Yeah, let's try Sergie," says Sam starting the car engine.

"Let's get a good start with getting there before it gets too busy. I think it will be alright if you turn your cell phone off," says Amanda.

"You got it, phone is off honey," says Sam turning his phone off in the car.

"Keep in touch with the road as you drive. Remember last time we almost got clipped by a semi," says Amanda.

"It was the semi's fault, I had enough distance from it and I had the right away," says Sam.

"Right away, there is no right away with a semi. Notice that traffic revolves around the movement of a semi and other transport vehicles. The semi will always win," says Amanda.

"Yeah, you are right I do need to practice defensive driving a lot more," says Sam.

"Estimated time of arrival is ten minutes, there should be good parking available," says Amanda.

"There you go, you almost got the entire family killed again," says Amanda.

"What, what did I do?" says Sam.

"The person turning across oncoming traffic almost hit us," says Amanda.

"There is nothing I could have done about that," says Sam continuing to drive through the intersection.

"I know I'm just trying to let you know of our current situation," says Amanda.

"Our current situation is no different," says Sam.

"Sometimes things change," says Amanda.

Upon arrival at the restaurant, the parking lot has a hand full of spaces open. The entrance to the building has a long waiting line. In many cases the people have to wait a half hour for a table to open up. Due to their small party, the couple did not have to wait long.

"Okay here are your menus. My name is Tina and will be your waitress today, would you like anything right away?" says Tina.

"Yes, I will have a Coke with a side salad to start," says Sam.

"I will have a Pepsi," says Amanda.

"I will be right back with those items," says Tina writing notes on her writing pad.

"Okay, back in the car we were talking about a change in our current situation," says Sam.

"Yes, back to the topic, I have something to share with you," says Amanda.

"Okay let's start with the good news first then the bad

news. If possible, try the sandwich approach of good news, bad news, and again some more good news," says Sam.

"There's only good news," says Amanda.

"Even better," says Sam.

"Sam I'm pregnant," says Amanda with a blush in her cheeks.

As if time slowed suddenly, Sam raises his eyebrows and takes into account the true meaning of what she is saying.

"Even better, it's better than ever," says Sam.

"The best way to figure out the change this means to us is taking the steps necessary to be prepared for this new child," says Amanda.

"This is a great way to start our evening and enjoy the moment we have been waiting for," says Sam.

"To me, this is the next progression to take in our lives. Where do you think we are headed? And is it the necessary steps to take in order to be where we want to be?" says Amanda.

"The process of getting to where we want to be will have surprises, a person will always have detours," says Sam.

"Do you mean like the time we tried to paint the kitchen and put wall paper up? It took us twice as long as expected," says Amanda.

"A perfect example, yeah the rug rat of the century is going to be in our hands," says Sam.

"Most of my concern comes from how we will delegate responsibility for taking care of the child and which values to instill," says Amanda.

"Let's enjoy the evening and not worry about that right now," says Sam.

"Well, have you decided what to order?" says Tina approaching the table with a pen and writing pad in hand.

"Yes, I will have the rib eye with swiss mushroom sauce," says Amanda.

"I'll have the same," says Sam.

Tina, the waitress writes the two menu choices down on her pad on what seems to be only a few letters scribbled. Moving away from the table, Tina maneuvers kitty corner from where they're seated to the next table waiting for a bill.

"I love the way this is turning out to be, can't wait to instill values in a child of my own. Just like a farmer planting seeds and watching them grow," says Sam.

"A person definitely reaps what they sow, which is something I think you will be good at showing," says Amanda.

"Today's children are a little smarter, the minute a person tries to give them direction, they will challenge it and quite possibly improve upon what you already know," says Sam.

"I agree, evolution in the making," says Amanda.

***

Three months later….

"Hi, my name is Amanda, we have an appointment for an ultra sound at eleven today with Dr. Brunner," says Amanda.

"Yes, Dr. Brunner will be right with you," says the receptionist.

"How long do you think it will take?" says Sam.

"About thirty minutes at most, at least that is what Macy said about her ultra sound," says Amanda.

"Amanda," says a Doctor looking around the waiting area.

Raising her hand, Amanda stands up and walks toward the doctor with Sam following behind just a few steps.

"Amanda, how has your day been? Any big highlights since we met last month?" says Dr. Brunner.

"Nothing big, just getting bigger by the day," says Amanda.

"I'm sure Sam has something more to say about your experiences," says Dr. Brunner.

"My best experience has been mediating the mood swings," says Sam.

"My mood isn't so bad is it?" says Amanda.

"That would be from a change of hormone levels occurring during pregnancy. Don't take it to heart what she tells you sometimes Sam," says Dr. Brunner.

"Oh, like when she was helping me fold laundry, telling me how I forgot to make the arm fold on t-shirts before making the last half fold. Later, I was informed my posture while bending over to pick up the laundry was improper by bending at the waist instead of hinging at the hips," says Sam.

"I bet you have a great opportunity to put Sam to work now that he is doing most of the work around the house Amanda," says Dr. Brunner.

The walk takes them all the way back to the end of the hall into a dim lit room. There is an exam bed, two chairs and an office chair for Dr. Brunner.

"Now let's get you set up, I will be applying a cream

on your abdomen Amanda. Then I will run the machine and get the picture of your new baby onto the screen. From there, we can tell the gender," says Dr. Brunner

"Okay, let's see what we find, and we would like to know the gender," says Amanda.

"Ah, I have some news," says Dr. Brunner looking up at the computer screen.

"Is the baby okay?" says Amanda.

"There's more than one baby," says Dr. Brunner.

"Wow, amazing honey did you hear that?" says Amanda looking at Sam in surprise.

"Yeah, looks like we will be busy with two kids," says Sam.

"Well looks like everything is alright, by the way, they're both girls," says Dr. Brunner.

"Well, there should be some drama unexpectedly occurring in our household. How do I get around providing each child equal amounts of attention?" says Sam.

"That is always the case with children; a person must do to one what they do to the other. I will schedule another appointment for you next month so I can check to see how you are progressing," says Dr. Brunner.

***

Six months later….

"Amanda, remember those Kegel exercises we did? Now relax and push we almost have the baby delivered," says the nurse.

"Push, Push," says Amanda in a whisper, trying to focus all her energy on delivering the baby.

"You can do it Amanda, this is the moment you've been waiting for," says Sam.

"A little more," says Dr. Brunner.

"Did you hear that Amanda, almost there a little more," says Sam.

The birth of the two babies occur a few minutes apart with both being girls like the doctor said.

"I was coming up with names from this book and do Jamie and Janice ring a bell?" says Sam looking in a baby name book.

"How about Kate and Kimberly?" says Amanda.

"Hey, that sounds good, let's go with that," says Sam.

"Sam, if you were to give our children one thing what would it be?" says Amanda.

"Hard decision, I would choose between a strong family bond, a religious affiliation, and a post secondary education," says Sam with a focused look on Kate and Kimberly.

"Why not give all those things to them in their lifetime, we can do it," says Amanda.

CHAPTER 18

"Hi this is Amanda," says Amanda answering the phone.

"Yes, Amanda I have some unfortunate news to say. Your grandfather Tom passed away this morning from a heart attack," says Barney.

Pausing frozen on the phone line, Amanda is in shock upon hearing about the death of her grand father Tom.

"Oh dad, I'm so sorry I know he was the person you always looked up to and I'm having difficulty finding words to describe what this loss means," says Amanda.

"Tom was the first person I knew who could take an idea and flip it inside out so he could start working from the end to back to the beginning. He's the one who inspired me to start my business you know," says Barney.

"When will the funeral be?" says Amanda.

"The funeral is going to take place on Wednesday at eleven in the morning we will meet at the church around nine," says Barney.

"Okay see you there, bye," says Amanda hanging up the phone.

***

Wednesday morning all the family and friends gather at a

church to pay their last visit to Tom. After many years of hard work and dedication to building the family name, Tom can now be laid to rest.

"When I was in college failing my accounting classes, dad would harp on me to hit the books and be all that I could be in the face of failure. I told him that I was going to fail the class anyway and his response was about me having the wrong attitude. That a person wasn't considered a failure until they fell down and didn't get back up," says Barney talking to some of Tom's old friends from the past years.

"Sounds like Tom, never afraid to keep going when no possible solution exists. You know, one time he saved me in a real big pickle. I was at fault for a car accident for running a red light and crashing into a nice Ford Mustang. The owner of the Mustang looked like he was about to kill me with his tire iron. Thankfully, Tom negotiated with him about some services that I could offer him in his home restoration to pay it back," says an old gentleman.

"That is great to hear, I wish you well in the coming years and may Tom live in each of us always," says Amanda moving towards Barney and his group engaged in conversation.

"How much did Grandpa Tom leave in his will for the family?" says Amanda.

"We will cover that tonight, for now, let's celebrate Grandpa's life and all the memories he leaves behind," says Barney with a depressed look on his face.

"Of course, have you seen your brother Dale?" says Amanda.

"Dale could not make it with the storm on the East Coast delaying all flights the past couple of days. I'm sure he will come as soon as possible," says Barney.

With about one hundred people attending Grandpa Tom's funeral, all were sad to see such a self made man go away. Getting through the great depression and later using most of his life's savings towards his sons business ventures was a risk at the time. Dale started a home cleaning service that never thrived in the three years of operation and Barney going from repairing lawn mowers and tractors to transitioning the business into tire production. Today, that tire producer is known as Landstrom Tires.

"Okay dad, are you finally going to get a good night's sleep tonight?" says Amanda.

"Yes, looking at his will, over a million will be split by Dale and I. Sixty grand will go to each grandchild and that's it. There is two grandchildren on Dale's side and only you on my side," whispers Barney realizing Amanda won't stop interrupting his conversation until he discloses what's in Tom's will.

"Wow, how does that get dispersed to me?" says Amanda.

"I was talking to dad's financial advisor just now and they can either keep the money where it is or pay taxes and do with the money what you please. Here is a contact number for you to speak with the advisor if needed," says Barney handing the advisor's business card to Amanda.

"I would sure like to pay down some debt," says Amanda.

"Ah, those high interest credit cards have gotten me before," says Barney.

"What would you do with the money at my age," says Amanda.

Pausing to do some deep thinking, Barney comes up with an answer.

"I would brainstorm possible ways a person could put that money towards and pick the best three choices. With these three choices, I would put a third of the money to each. Of course when I was your age, I should have used it all to buy Kunnings stock which grew more than Microsoft over the years," says Barney.

"That's a good idea, I will try to invest in my future," says Amanda.

'Instead of saying, "I will try," say, "I will," it's going to happen,' says Barney.

"I love what they've done with grandpa's coffin, looks like it's made out of marble," says Amanda.

"Indeed it is made out of marble, the finest in the U.S. Speaking of marbles, Andrew I bet you played a game of marbles with my father," says Barney turning to Andrew, a black haired man with no facial hair in a suit and tie.

"We go back to those childhood days, you are right, I always could outlast Tom in school, but once we got out his talents really took off," says Andrew with his bald head and black hair on the sides.

"Well, you are in great condition and health Andrew," says Barney.

"You see, my face is old and quite wrinkled, but my eyes are of that of a baby. I still have a lot of life in my eyes and a spring in my step," says Andrew with his brown eyes wide to show them clearly.

"I'm wondering if Tom would have agreed to that?" says Amanda.

"We never could agree on much, maybe, it was just

his way of finding more possibilities and diversity," says Andrew.

"Now, excuse us Andrew. The funeral is about to get under way," says Barney.

At the opening of the funeral ceremony, the immediate family sat in front facing Priest Sanders and the Tom's coffin situated in between. Red and white flowers filled the floor in front of the coffin with a portrait of Tom in his early twenties to the coffin's right.

'Now, it always amazed me that Tom was either behind the pack or ahead of the pack, I guess he wasn't comfortable doing what everyone else was doing. For example, when being behind the pack he would respond to me. "I'm looking for a better way to remember my losses in life". When being in front of the pack he would respond to me, "I'm looking for a way to disperse all that I have so that it does the most good." I don't think Tom was comfortable being behind or ahead of the pack for very long,' says Priest Sanders.

Towards the end of the priest's speech, half of the immediate family is in tears with a gut wrenching hold eating at each of them from the inside out.

'Back at the end of the pack, I think Tom secretly didn't mind it a bit. I know with his half squinting eyes of confidence he will say, "I learned the most back here and everything is ahead of me."'

With each aisle exiting the church having immediate family leaving first, the mile to the cemetery for the burial was a slow drive even in mid-day traffic. Amazingly, most of the people for the funeral ceremony also attended the burial. The mild late winter day made the shaded canopy cool with blocking the sun light.

"Did you find out about the estate left by Tom?" says Sam driving back home from the funeral.

"Yes, about sixty grand is in it for me, which I'm going to disperse evenly to debt reduction, a college fund for the kids, and some retirement money," say Amanda.

"Not a bad idea, definitely dispersing your money will reduce your risk. I have a friend at work who brags about getting fourteen percent a year from the interest accruing on his stock picks. Are you interested in something like that?" says Sam.

"That sounds like a great idea; I want to do with this money what I previously said earlier. When I do get some extra cash though, I want to go ahead and get into what that co-worker is doing. A person doesn't hear of a consistent fourteen percent gain," says Amanda.

"What do we have to lose? The way I see it, pushing the risk now is going to grow our capital like a weed. The occupations we have are fairly secure and family owned. Keep chunking in the change and a showcase of Benjamin's will be the result," says Sam.

Chapter 19

"Hutchinson Investments, this is Janice," says Janice.

"Hi Janice, this is Amanda I just had some questions regarding my portfolio results these past few years," says Amanda.

"Yeah, sure what are you looking to ask?" says Janice.

"My profit gains have averaged eight percent these past few years, do you think there is a different option to get more profit gains?" says Amanda.

"The plan we are currently on is experiencing a low period and should bounce into the teens when congress passes this new bill for securities in the U.S.," says Janice.

"I'm looking for better options and I know they are out there," says Amanda.

"We have to be weary some of those options are extremely volatile and too good to be true. What are you considering on doing?" says Janice.

"I know of an investment right now that is gaining fourteen percent a year consistently," says Amanda.

"The stock market is always changing and I bet that fourteen percent is not going to remain for long due to the checks and balances of the market. Think of it as the economy with inflation, GDP, and the unemployment rate never sitting at a stand still for an extended period of time.

For example, the last time our inflation was at today's level we were back in the 70's. Considering this same inflation rate, our GDP and unemployment is different now than back in the 70's," says Janice.

"I want more gains and have decided to take my money elsewhere. Transfer my account monies over to Dunlevy's, my account number there is 123454321," says Amanda.

"I will do that for you, but for your information, did you know you will pay a third in taxes on your gains?" says Janice.

"Yes, I'm aware of that, but I will make up for that third in six years with fourteen percent gains at Dunlevy's," says Amanda.

"I will transfer it over as soon as possible. I enjoyed working with you and wish you the best," says Janice.

"Yes, thanks for your cooperation and work," says Amanda hanging up the phone while sitting in her office at work.

"Oh Amanda, has there been a decision about what to do with your part of Tom's inheritance?" says Barney standing next to Amanda's office door.

"Yes, I'm going to put it into an investment gaining fourteen percent consistently," says Amanda.

"Fourteen percent is unheard of for the long term, what's the secret?" says Barney curious with eyebrows high on his forehead.

"I know, but I'm too comfortable right now with what I'm doing. You know more than I do about risk being necessary for significant growth," says Amanda.

"I agree, try it and learn as much as you can from your

decision because you are entering into uncharted waters," says Barney.

"I think why not give it a try," says Amanda.

"Tom would have agreed with your decision. Don't forget about the meeting tomorrow afternoon," says Barney walking away to his next task.

Looking up at the framed poster of a climber scaling the side of a mountain, next to her office window, Amanda reads the one word and definition below:

"*Change-*
To make the form, nature, content, future course, etc, of something different from what it is or what it would be if left alone."

"That's an awful definition for change, how about, an uncomfortable feeling when progressing for improvement in an unusual situation," says Amanda to herself.

Taking a few minutes to gaze at the poster and perfecting the definition to her personal meaning of change. As the day draws on for Amanda, she hits a wall about two thirty in the afternoon and decides to head for the break room for some coffee. Noticing the break room being full, she waits in a line of four people to get her cup of coffee.

"Hey Amanda, I really admire the work that you do," says a short brunette woman in her forties.

"Thanks, what department are you in?" says Amanda.

"Janitorial, my name is Carla," says Carla.

Getting a cup of coffee by filling half the cup with coffee and half with cream, Carla holds the pot of coffee up at arms length to pour Amanda a cup. Amanda's hand holding the cup shakes slightly displaying nervousness.

"What is your mind set for achieving all that success in your life?" says Carla.

"My mind set is taking all I can get so I can give all that I have," says Amanda.

"I don't know if I could ever adopt that mind set, Amanda," says Carla.

"Why not?" says Amanda sipping her coffee.

"The smaller my life is and the less materials I have, the happier I' am," says Carla.

"It's natural for a person to always want more, to always want better. You shouldn't try to hide it," says Amanda.

"The more I want, the less control there is in being fortunate for what I already have," says Carla.

"Pick your poison, always wanting more or never having enough, which I see wanting more as being optimistic and never having enough as being pessimistic," says Amanda.

"I see your point of view, isn't always wanting more and never having enough saying the same thing. Except an individual never having enough puts a stop to the materialistic ideology," says Carla.

"Great point, I can see where they are both the same with each having different wording," says Amanda with wide glaring eyes.

"I have to go, nice speaking with you," says Carla.

"Yep, and the same to you Carla," says Amanda.

On the way back to the office, Amanda gives a sigh of relief to almost being done with her current tire sales project. Setting her cup of coffee on her desk, the phone rings and Amanda goes to pick up the phone.

"Amanda here," says Amanda.

"Yeah, will the new tire sales results be reported tomorrow? I would really want to know what the sales peak might be for tomorrow," says Barney on the phone.

"I'm almost certain the sales results will be ready by then," says Amanda.

"Great, I'm anxious to see where the numbers stand on this tire's life cycle," says Barney.

"Dad, I have a call on the other line, can I put you on hold?" says Amanda.

"Yes, no need calling me back, I have no more to cover," says Barney hanging up the phone.

Amanda repositions herself in the chair so that her other hip is bearing the most weight and pushes the button on the phone for the other line.

"Hi, Amanda here," says Amanda.

"Yes, this is Lillete at Dunlevy's, we have confirmed a transfer of money from Hutchinson Investments today, is there a certain way you want this money invested Amanda?" says Lillete.

Yes, there is a fund right now that is making fourteen percent consistently; I would like to put three-fourths of the money into that fund, with the remaining money going into the index fund that you have," says Amanda.

"Great choice, I bet you're talking of the Balcom New World Growth and Dividend Fund," says Lillete.

"If it has been performing as well as people are saying I want in," says Amanda.

"At thirty-six point nine a share your sixty grand will get one thousand six hundred and sixty two shares. The remaining twenty grand will be put into the index fund with one thousand and seventeen shares. I'd say it would provide for a hefty retirement," says Lillete.

"I'm also looking to purchase some individual stock, do you have any suggestions? How about borrowing money with a stock margin loan? " says Amanda.

"Yes, a good place to start is by buying reputable growing companies that you have interest in and buying when the stock is at a fifty two week below average price," says Lillete.

"I have five thousand to invest today. I like Arnex stock, which is at a fifty-two week low," says Amanda.

"Arnex looks to be a great idea, with five grand you can purchase up to ten grand in Arnex stock with the margin loan. The interest rate is 2.5 percent and the margin call will be a stock price of twenty-five percent less than today's price per share, which is forty-two thirty-five," says Lillete.

Yes, go ahead and do the ten grand margin call and I will stop into your office after work to finalize the investment," says Amanda.

"Interesting, I love to get bargains on sale, especially when I can borrow more for a better return. I have to get on to my next appointment. People seem to go through tires as if they are a NASCAR driver," says Amanda.

"Okay, I'll see you this afternoon, talk to you soon," says Lillete ending the conversation.

***

"You what?" says Sam.

"I did a margin loan last year with some Arnex stock and now my broker gave a margin call saying the stock has dipped a third and more money is needed to keep the investment alive. I'm really tight with money right now, can you put some in my account at Dunlevy's?" says Amanda.

"Risky, please let me know what you are doing from now on so that I have some preparation for the worse case scenario," says Sam.

"I need $3,300 to fulfill my margin call or they will sell some shares to keep up with money owed," says Amanda.

"Yeah, I will transfer some from my business savings tomorrow morning, but stick with this margin loan. This investment might take off in a short period of time with this growing company," says Sam.

"Thanks sweety, but I'm not sure if this company is growing right now," says Amanda before giving Sam a quick kiss on the lips.

Amanda and Sam continue eating supper at the dinner table with feelings of having the problem solved for a clear plan in place to overcome this temporary setback. Perhaps, the well lit dining area provides a helpful atmosphere for problem solving.

***

"Wow!" says Amanda looking at the price of Arnex stock during her lunch.

"Just six months ago I was in a margin call and now it's about doubled. I've got to capitalize on this," says Amanda.

Grabbing the phone, Amanda calls Dunlevy's.

"Dunlevy's Investments, this is Trisha speaking," says Trisha.

"Yes, my name is Amanda, is Lillete available right now?" says Amanda.

"One moment while I put you on hold," says Trisha.

Pausing the call with Madonna music playing in the background, Lillete picks up after about a thirty second hold.

"Lillete speaking," says Lillete picking up the phone.

"Lillete this is Amanda, the Arnex margin loan I have is at high price right now. Would you suggest on selling right now at eighty-two forty one a share?" says Amanda.

"I agree, there is no guarantee that it will rise further, I will sell at the opening price tomorrow. This loan turned out to be worth over nine grand for you, talk about timing the market right," says Lillete.

"Give all I can to get all I can," says Amanda.

Chapter 20

"So now, some ten years later I happen to meet you at this coffee shop for us to tell each other about our own journey after college," says Roy.

"It took us long enough, it must be two in the afternoon by now, I should really get going," says Amanda.

"I don't know if I've said this before, but I guess I wouldn't have had it any other way. You see, I've always worked twice as hard as the next person to reach an achievement. Is this due to destiny with the situation I was born into as coming from a low socioeconomic family? Maybe, I surely wasn't given what I have today," says Roy.

"How come you seem to work so hard, earn so much, and live so frugally?" says Amanda.

"Is this what I value or is this part of what my vision is," says Roy.

"It's probably both value and vision. What do you see in this world that other people don't?" says Amanda.

"I see everyone's inflated expectations shrinking or coming true after being picked from the litter," says Roy.

"Jake, can I get another coffee? This is the third cup for me as you can see, I have a lot and can't control the use of it," says Amanda with two empty coffee cups on the table in front of her.

"Coming right up," says Jake getting up from his comfortable seat on the bar stool.

"In the end, we reap what we sow. In my grain fields, the crops need sun, water, and soil. Just like a person's needs, wants, and aspiring dreams, they rarely occur all at once," says Roy.

"I can see that, since when is it sunny and rainy at the same time?" says Amanda.

Walking over to the booth, Jake hands a perfectly blended mocha coffee to Amanda. Jake rotates to face Roy and gestures with palm up.

"Would you like anything else today?" says Jake.

"No thank you, can we get our receipt? This will be on one tab," says Roy.

"Surely," says Jake walking over to the cash register to tally up the receipt.

"Are you sure you will be able to drive home with all that sugar and caffeine?" says Roy.

"It shouldn't be a problem, actually, I should be more alert," says Amanda.

"Yeah, too alert," says Roy.

"So where do we go from here?" says Amanda.

"Go our separate ways with each of us giving all we have to offer this world because there is no greater fulfillment," says Roy.

Jake sets the receipt face down on the table with a pen on top between Roy and Amanda.

"Have a great day Roy, I'll see you tomorrow," says Jake walking back to his bar stool.

"You must be a regular," says Amanda.

"I'm here every day Amanda, I own the place," says Roy.

"What? That doesn't sound like you, take care Roy," says Amanda getting out of the booth.

"Never underestimate the power of living below ones means. Feel free to stop in again sometime," says Roy.

"If I'm in the neighborhood," says Amanda breaking eye contact with Roy while turning around and heading out the front door.

There is a silent period after Amanda leaves. With the traffic outside starting to calm down, the noon rush hour is over and no one is present in the shop. This looks to be the best time of the day for a person to prepare for the next rush after three. Roy walks down the bar aisle into the back room where Jake is doing dishes.

"How many transactions today Jake?" says Roy.

"One twenty-one and counting boss, this is better than Chester's Chicken, huh?" says Jake.

"Yes, we're ahead of the quota for the day," says Roy.

"I remember you working at Chester's years ago," says Jake.

"Huh, that's odd, I don't remember you," says Roy.

"That's because I owned the place at the time," says Jake.

"What are you doing working here Jake?" says Roy.

"Just here for the experience," says Jake.

"Who owns Chester's Chicken now?" says Roy.

"I do," says Jake.

"Why are you working here then?" says Roy.

"To give me something to do and most of all to serve others. Maybe, taking position behind the pack is all I care about," says Jake with a big smile on his face.

About the Author

After having many encounters with peoples pursuit to live a meaningful and successful life, I have identified various ways people achieve what they want. I'm in the same boat with many others for the pursuit of work after a post secondary education. What I see everyone else face allows me to relate to my own personal experiences and sharing those experiences makes everyone better. I currently live in West Fargo, North Dakota. One of the most important lessons in my life is that an individual will get out what they put in.